"David!" Wishbone called
as he rushed back
toward his friend.

"We have to beat it out of here! I'm trying to escape what is just beyond those trees!" Wishbone said in a state of panic.

"What are you afraid of?" David knelt beside the dog.

"Them!" Wishbone said, pointing his muzzle toward the Peabodys. "I think they're coming after me!"

Books in The Adventures of WiSHBONe™ series:

Be a Wolf!
Salty Dog
The Prince and the Pooch
Robinhound Crusoe
Hunchdog of Notre Dame
Digging Up the Past
The Mutt in the Iron Muzzle
Muttketeer!
A Tale of Two Sitters
Moby Dog
The Pawloined Paper
Dog Overboard!
Homer Sweet Homer
Dr. Jekyll and Mr. Dog
A Pup in King Arthur's Court
The Last of the Breed
Digging to the Center of the Earth
Gullifur's Travels
Terrier of the Lost Mines
Ivanhound
Huckleberry Dog
Twenty Thousand Wags Under the Sea*

Books in The Super Adventures of WiSHBONe™ series:

Wishbone's Dog Days of the West
The Legend of Sleepy Hollow
Unleashed in Space
Tails of Terror

*coming soon

The Adventures of WISHBONE™

HUCKLEBERRY DOG

by Alexander Steele

Inspired by *Adventures of Huckleberry Finn*
by Mark Twain

WISHBONE™ created by Rick Duffield

Big Red Chair Books™, *A Division of **Lyrick Publishing**™*

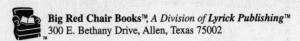 **Big Red Chair Books**™, *A Division of Lyrick Publishing*™
300 E. Bethany Drive, Allen, Texas 75002

©2000 Big Feats! Entertainment

Cover concept and design by Lyle Miller

Interior illustrations by Kathryn Yingling

Wishbone photograph by Carol Kaelson

Library of Congress Catalog Card Number: 99-63427

ISBN: 1-57064-389-X

First printing: March 2000

10 9 8 7 6 5 4 3 2 1

This book is dedicated to you, the reader.
Without you, none of us would be here right now.

FROM THE BIG RED CHAIR . . .

Oh...hi! Wishbone here. You caught me right in the middle of some of my favorite things—books. Let me welcome you to THE ADVENTURES OF WISHBONE. In each of these books, I have adventures with my friends in Oakdale and imagine myself as a character in one of the greatest stories of all time. This story takes place in the summer, when Joe is twelve—during the first season of my television show.

In *HUCKLEBERRY DOG*, I imagine I'm fourteen-year-old Huckleberry Finn, a plain ol' country boy from Mark Twain's ***ADVENTURES OF HUCKLEBERRY FINN.*** It's about the journey of a boy and a slave on the mighty Mississippi River during the 1800s.

You're in for a real treat, so pull up a chair, grab a snack, and sink your teeth into *HUCKLEBERRY DOG!*

Chapter One

Wishbone lay in the grass, feeling the summer sun warm his back. A soft breeze blew by, ruffling the dog's white fur with brown and black spots. On a lazy Saturday like this, the backyard felt like a paradise.

Ah, this is the life, the Jack Russell terrier thought. *No cares, no clouds. No Wanda Gilmore yelling at me about digging through her flower garden next door. Let's see . . . I've spent some time resting in the shade and I've spent some time resting in the sun. What's next on my busy schedule? Oh, I know.*

Wishbone trotted to the back of the house and entered through his own personal doggie door. Pen in hand, Ellen Talbot, the lady of the house, was busy making a grocery list in the kitchen.

"Do you know what time it is?" Wishbone asked Ellen. "I'll give you a hint. It starts with "snack" and it ends with "time.""

Wishbone waited a moment, but Ellen didn't answer.

"Give up?" Wishbone said, rising onto his hind legs. "Okay, I'll tell you the answer. It's snacktime!"

"I think we need mustard," Ellen said, opening the refrigerator.

And doggie treats! Wishbone thought.

But Ellen wrote only the word "mustard" on the list. *Why is it she never listens to the dog?* Wishbone wondered, dropping to all fours. *Ellen is a great mother, but she isn't always on top of the all-important food issues.*

Ellen's son, Joe Talbot, entered the kitchen. He was a good-natured twelve-year-old boy with straight brown hair and a great smile. Wishbone shared a room with Joe, and they were the very best friends.

"We need cookies," Joe said, pulling two ginger-snaps from the cookie jar. He slid one in his mouth and let the other slip quietly to the floor. In a snap, Wishbone gobbled up the treat.

"Thanks, pal," Wishbone told Joe. "I'm glad someone around here has his priorities straight."

"I saw that," Ellen said without looking up from her list. "But I'll get more cookies."

The doorbell rang, and Ellen turned away to answer it.

Mindful of his role as house watchdog, Wishbone followed Ellen through the hallway. The door opened, revealing a man and woman waiting on the front porch. They seemed to be about Ellen's age. The slender woman wore her hair coiled on her head and a silky scarf around her neck. A wide leather purse was dangling from her arm. The man, dressed in a dark suit with a shirt and tie, was carrying a fat suitcase. Their pasted-on smiles made Wishbone a little nervous.

"Good morning," Ellen greeted the couple.

"Hello," the woman said, her voice chipper as a bird call. "I'm Mrs. Flora Peabody and this is my husband Frank. Do you by any chance own a dog?"

Wishbone stepped into view. "Yes, I live here, if that's what you mean."

"That answers my first question." Mrs. Peabody reached down to pat Wishbone's head. "What a handsome Jack Russell."

"His name is Wishbone," Ellen said. "How can I help you?"

"My husband and I have started a special line of clothing—doggie clothing." Mrs. Peabody's eyes sparkled with enthusiasm. "Most of our sales are through mail order. But now and then, we go door to door. Catalogs and the Internet are terrific selling tools, but we miss the personal contact with our customers."

"Absolutely," Mr. Peabody agreed.

"Sounds interesting," Ellen told the couple. "But Wishbone doesn't wear clothing."

"No self-respecting dog wears clothing," Wishbone muttered. "If we dogs wanted to dress up, we would have been born human."

But Mrs. Peabody didn't seem to hear. "Queenie!" Distracted, she called toward the hedges on the side of the house. "Come here! You'll tear your tutu."

"Who's Queenie?" Wishbone asked.

Then . . . a creature appeared on the porch. At first glance, Wishbone thought it was something from an alien planet, but he soon realized it was only a little poodle. Her snow-white fur was sculpted, the way it's

9

trimmed at expensive dog salons. Two pink ribbons decorated the dog's head, and she wore a pink tutu — a ballerina outfit with sequins and a frilly skirt. *That is one ridiculous-looking dog,* thought Wishbone.

"This is our little Queenie," Mrs. Peabody said, proudly.

"Oh, my," Ellen said with a surprised expression, "that outfit is . . . really something."

"Just part of our collection." Mr. Peabody gave his suitcase a proud tap. "Care to take a look at some of our clothes?"

"Thanks, but no thanks," Wishbone muttered to himself.

"Uh, well . . . " Ellen hesitated.

"If you're busy, we can come back," Mrs. Peabody offered.

"No," Ellen said, trying to be polite. "I doubt that I'll buy anything, but I'd be happy to take a look."

The visitors marched right into the living room, where Joe was sitting. He glanced up from behind a magazine. As Ellen introduced him, he shot a surprised look at Queenie's odd attire.

"I feel the same way," Wishbone whispered to Joe.

"We call ourselves Canine Couture," Mr. Peabody set the suitcase on the sofa and popped it open. Colorful fabrics spilled out. "Fun fashions for furry friends. Every item is handmade."

"Please," Mrs. Peabody said, "don't be shy. And while you're looking, would you mind if I used your restroom?"

"Of course not," Ellen said. "Joe, why don't you show her—"

"No, no, just tell me where it is," Mrs. Peabody said. "I don't want to bother anyone."

"Just down the hall," Ellen said, pointing the way.

As Mrs. Peabody headed off, Wishbone moved toward the suitcase for a better look. Queenie bared her teeth, growling.

"Queenie thinks all the clothes belong to her," Mr. Peabody explained. "She gets jealous when other dogs come too close."

Hey, she's welcome to the whole suitcase, Wishbone thought, taking a seat on the floor near Joe. *I've said it before and I'll say it again. No self-respecting dog wears clothing!*

Mr. Peabody pulled several sweaters from the suitcase and laid them on the sofa. "One hundred percent wool! And we have some stunning designs, mostly for fall and winter, of course."

I'll wear it when we have a snowstorm in July.

Ellen eyed the sweaters, nodding her head.

Uh-oh. Ellen can't be thinking about buying this stuff.

"And if you're looking for something more unique," Mr. Peabody continued, "look no further than this." He whipped out a zebra-striped jacket with a black velvet collar. It looked like something a model might wear in the pages of a fashion magazine.

Queenie scurried over for a closer look. Her tail wagged eagerly, sticking out of the back of her pink tutu.

"That would be for female dogs, right?" Ellen asked.

"It's for male or female," Mr. Peabody said. "It's European."

11

Fine, save it for some Belgian sheepdog.

Mrs. Peabody reappeared with the same bright smile. "If you're looking for something more masculine, how about this?" She held up a black leather jacket with a red emblem on the back. Ellen reached over to feel the leather.

Wishbone lowered his muzzle. *Could Ellen be interested?*

"Joe, take a look at this," Ellen urged.

Joe checked out the jacket. "This one is pretty cool."

Wishbone blinked in shock. *No, no, no. Say it ain't so, Joe!*

"And these are for casual, dress-down days," Mrs. Peabody said, pulling out several T-shirts.

"Look at the logos, Joe." Ellen held up one shirt after another. "'Paws Up!' And 'Doggie Garbage Disposal.'"

Joe held up another and laughed. "'Pooch University.'"

Wishbone gave his ear a scratch. *I can't believe what I'm hearing. Have Ellen and Joe lost it? If they buy these clothes, guess what poor dog is going to be wearing them? Totally against his will, of course.*

"Isn't this adorable?" Mrs. Peabody dangled a yellow rain slicker that came with a matching cap.

Ellen smiled. "It is cute."

Adorable? Cute? Not on my fur! Wishbone thought with growing panic. *I won't be able to show my face to Sparky and all the other neighborhood dogs. I'll be howled out of the park. Even the squirrels and ducks will laugh at me. This is a disaster!*

"And this," Mrs. Peabody said, presenting a tuxedo complete with bowtie and pink carnation, "we call 'Dog on the Town.'"

Try Dog out of Town, Wishbone thought, scrambling to his feet. *Okay, that does it. I can't stick around for dress-ups. I have no choice. Time to escape. At least until this fashion frenzy blows over. Adios, amigos!*

Wishbone darted from the living room, following the familiar route to his doggie door. He wasn't sure where he was going, but he had to get away. He needed to protect his natural good looks, his doggie dignity, and his freedom!

Sweet freedom, that's what it's all about. That reminds me of one of my all-time favorite stories. It's a book about about a young boy who ran away in search of his own kind of freedom.

The book was published in 1885 by that most famous of American authors, Mark Twain. No matter how old he grew, Mr. Twain never lost his spirit of adventure. And he packed his books with a lot of laughs, too.

Oh, I can almost see the story's hero floating down the river on a raft, getting himself into one crazy adventure after another. Yep, I'm thinking of that timeless tale, *Adventures of Huckleberry Finn!*

Chapter Two

Wishbone floated deep into his imagination. He pictured himself as Huckleberry Finn, a teenage boy who lived along the Mississippi River back in the early 1800s. Huckleberry told the story in his very own words.

Howdy,

You probably don't know about me unless you've read a book called *The Adventures of Tom Sawyer*. I'm a character in that book, which was also written by Mr. Mark Twain. He stretched the facts some, here and there, but mainly he told the truth. Don't worry if you haven't already read that book. I'll catch you up on everything you need to know.

First off, my name is Huckleberry Finn. A lot of folks call me Huck, and that's fine too. I'm just a plain ol' country boy, creeping up on my fourteenth year. I'm nothing special to look at, maybe just a bit shorter than the average kid my age. Even though I ain't respectable or educated, I do have my talents. I'm pretty good at fishing the river and whittling a piece of wood. And my little black nose can pick up a scent, even if it's coming from clear across the county.

My story starts out in St. Petersburg, a riverside town in the state of Missouri. Though Missouri sits about in the middle of the country, it has more the feel of a southern state. That's because folks don't rush around too much and they speak with a drawl and some of them own slaves.

Now the way *The Adventures of Tom Sawyer* winds up is this. In the summertime, my friend, Tom Sawyer, and I found a bag of money that some robbers had hidden in a cave. So we got to keep that money, which was six thousand dollars apiece. Judge Thatcher, a real decent man, he put my share of the money in the bank for me. But every now and then he gave me some coins to buy things at the general store, like maybe a piece of beef jerky or something else to chew on.

I came from a dirt-poor family, but I didn't live with my parents. My mother died when I was just a pup, and I hadn't seen my father for a while. For the past year I had been living by myself, sleeping in a barrel and snooping around for food. All in all, it was a pretty comfortable life.

But right after the episode in the cave, the Widow Douglas declared me a lost lamb in need of guidance. So she took me on, like I was her own son. She was a kindly lady with gray hair, but boy oh boy, she was determined to civilize me. She made me go to school and say grace before I ate my supper. She also wanted me to wear store-bought clothes that scratched my fur.

And the Widow Douglas had all kinds of instructions for me.

"Huckleberry, make sure your shirt is buttoned all the way."

"Huckleberry, it's time to work on your lessons for school.

"My dear boy, try not to tear through your food so fast. It's just not civilized."

Miss Watson, the widow's unmarried sister, was also living under our roof. She was a skinny woman who wore a pair of spectacles that reminded me of goggles. Miss Watson kept an even closer watch on me than the Widow Douglas. I tried my best to please that lady, but it was impossible. Every time I moved a paw, she was shouting a new order at me.

"Don't put your feet on that sofa, Huckleberry!"

"It's time to read your Bible, Huckleberry!"

"Don't keep scratching that rug, Huckleberry!"

"Huckleberry Finn, stop digging holes in that garden!"

Miss Watson told me I had to choose where I wanted to end up after I was dead. If I led a good and decent life, she said, I'd end up in Heaven. Then I could wander around forever, strumming a harp and howling beautiful songs. But if I didn't lead a good and decent life, I'd end up in the other direction — way deep underground in that place where it's always hot. I'll give you a hint. The name of the place rhymes with "bell."

One autumn night, I heard the town clock sound its twelve midnight gongs. Then, just outside my bedroom window, I heard a faint "me-yow, me-yow." Fast as a flash, I leaped outside. I was mighty fond of chasing cats but that's not what I was going outside for. You see, "me-yow, me-yow" was a secret signal from my friend, Tom Sawyer.

Tom was a boy my own age, but unlike me, he came from a respectable family. Tom was the craftiest kid in the world. He had read so many fantastic adventure books it was like he had a whole library stashed away under his curly hair.

"Come on," Tom whispered. "We've got business to take care of. It's secret stuff, though, so keep real quiet."

Tom Sawyer lived for mysterious activities. Over the past year, he and I had been through quite a few hair-raising adventures together.

My hearing was extra sharp, so I lifted my furred ears to hear if anyone was about. The wind whispered through the trees, and way off, an owl made its who-whooing sound. Otherwise, the night was quiet as a graveyard.

Tom and I crept through the yard, being careful not to crunch any twigs. But then, catching my paw on a root, I tripped and accidentally gave a small yelp. Right away, Tom and I dropped to our bellies, in case anyone had heard me.

"Who's there?" a voice called.

Sure enough, a man was sitting in the kitchen doorway. By the kitchen candlelight, I could see it was Jim, the black slave owned by Miss Watson. Tom and I stayed frozen in place.

Jim stood up, trying to see through the darkness. He was almost close enough to touch my muzzle, but he didn't seem to see me. Pretty soon, my ear got to itching. Then the fur along my back got to itching. Then my tail began itching so bad it brought tears to my eyes. It's always like that. Itching comes at the worst possible time, like at the most serious part of a church service. After a while I was itching in eleven different places. I didn't dare lift a paw to scratch, though, for fear that might give me away.

Finally, Jim wandered back into the house. Tom and I bolted out of the yard. After we climbed over the fence, the two of us laughed like a pair of hyenas. By then, my itching had magically disappeared.

When we got to the bottom of the hill, Tom and I met with Joe Harper and Ben Rogers and a few other boys we knew. Tom led us to the outskirts of town, then through a hole into a dark and damp cave. The place was so spooky, it made my tail shiver.

"Now," Tom announced as we took seats on the rocky ground, "we're going to start a band of robbers and call it Tom Sawyer's Gang. This here cave will be our hideout. Everybody that wants to join the gang has got to take an oath, swearing that they'll never give away our secrets. And then we've all got to write our names in blood."

Everybody did what Tom said because he knew about this kind of business.

After the blood stuff was done, Ben Rogers said, "What are we going to rob? Cattle?"

"Nah," Tom said with a wave of his hand. "We are highwaymen. That means we put on masks, then stop stagecoaches and passersby on the road and then take people's watches and money. And some times we'll capture people and ransom them."

"Ransom? What's that?" one of the fellows asked.

"I don't know," Tom replied, "but it's what high-waymen do. I've seen it in some books."

"But how can we do it if we don't know what it is?" Ben Rogers wondered.

"I'm not sure," Tom said, "but we've got to do it. If we start doing things different from the books, everything will get all muddled up."

"But how can we do it *if we don't know what it is?*" Ben repeated.

I raised a paw. "That's a good question, Ben."

"Look," Tom said, getting a little impatient, "we'll just capture the people, then keep a close guard on them and then . . . we'll figure things out. Maybe I can find the answer in some books about pirates or Robin Hood or something like that."

At this point, little Timmy Barnes began to cry because he wanted to go home. Tom gave the boy five cents to keep quiet.

"Do we ransom women or just men?" Joe Harper asked.

Tom's eyes glowed a bit. "By jings, of course we ransom women. That's one of the best things about being a robber. We'll treat the women just as polite as pie. By and by, they'll fall in love with us and then they won't want to go home anymore."

Liking that idea, I gave my tail a few wags.

"I don't know about this," Ben Rogers said, scratching his head. "Mighty soon we'll have the cave so cluttered up with women, not to mention fellows waiting to be ransomed, that there won't be any room for the robbers."

Tom closed his eyes with frustration. "Everybody, just leave all the details to me. That's why I'm the boss of Tom Sawyer's Gang!"

So on we went being robbers for a month or so. We'd go charging out of the woods, using sticks as swords and brooms as rifles. We'd whoop and yell at folks who were taking hogs and carts of vegetables to market.

One time, however, Tom told us that he'd got secret information that a bunch of Spanish merchants were coming to town with a parade of elephants and camels and tons of diamonds and four hundred soldiers to keep guard. Everybody got real excited about robbing those merchants. When the big day came, all the gang members hid behind some trees at the top of the hill. We planned to run down the hill and ambush the parade when it passed by below.

Since I had the best hearing, everyone was watching me. Ears raised high, I listened intently for about half an hour. Finally, I heard footsteps trampling the grass in the distance. I gave a signal with my paw. The other gang members gripped their pretend-weapons. Then a group of people marched into view. But doggone it, there weren't no merchants or diamonds or camels or elephants or soldiers. It was just a pack of Sunday school children on a picnic with their instructor.

"I guess you got your information wrong," I told Tom.

"No, I didn't," Tom replied. "An evil magician must have ordered his genie to cast a spell at the last minute. That happens sometimes."

I gave my ear a thoughtful scratch. "Say, Tom, how does a person get a genie anyway?"

"By rubbing an old tin lamp," Tom explained. "Then a genie, tall as a tree, appears in a midst of thunder and smoke. And then that genie's got to do whatever his master wants him to do."

"Anything?"

"Yep, anything. If you tell the genie to build a palace forty miles long and fill it full of chewing gum, he's got to do it. And it's got to be done by sunup the next morning."

"Well, if I was a genie," I said, "I wouldn't want to be running around doing everything I was told to do."

"If you're a genie, you've got to," Tom insisted. "Whether you want to or not!"

I rose up on my four paws. "Hey, if I was tall as a tree, I wouldn't have to do anything!"

"Shucks," Tom said, shaking his head sadly. "Huck Finn, you just don't understand how these things work."

Finally, I quit the robber gang. I began to realize that the whole thing was nothing but a bunch of pretending. Besides, I'm not sure I cared so much for robbing and ransoming folks in the first place.

Another three or four months ran along, taking us well into winter. All this time, I had been going to school because of the Widow Douglas. I learned to spell and read and write a little. And I'd gotten far enough in the multiplication tables to know six times seven is thirty-five.

I was getting sort of used to school and life with the Widow. I liked my old ways better but the new ones weren't so bad. The Widow said I was getting myself civilized, slow but sure, and she wasn't ashamed of me.

As the snow fell outside one night, I climbed upstairs to my bedroom. When I passed through the door, I almost jumped out of my fur in fright. My father was sitting in a chair, waiting for me.

I used to live with my father, or Pap as I called him, but I hadn't seen him for more than a year. And that was just fine by me. There was only two things Pap Finn was any good at—getting drunk and treating me rough.

Yes sir, my Pap was a mean man. He looked it, too.

His hair hung down, long and black and greasy, like tangled vines. His skin was pale as a fishbelly, and his clothes were nothing more than rags. He had one ankle resting on his other knee, and I could see several toes sticking out of the tip of his big boot.

For a few moments, I stared up at Pap, not saying anything. He stared down at me, just wriggling those exposed toes.

Finally Pap grumbled, "Look at them fancy clothes you wear, all stiff with starch. I bet you think you're better than your Pap now, don't you?"

"That's not true," I said, trying to sound real nice.

Pap raised a hand as he leaned forward. "Don't give me none of your sass, boy, or I'll smack you around good."

I kept my mouth shut. I had felt that big hand smack me too many times to forget.

"I understand you've been going to school," Pap grumbled. "Let me hear you read something."

I went to one of my school books and nervously opened it with my muzzle. After I struggled through a few sentences, Pap leaped from his chair. He snatched the book away and threw it hard against the wall.

"Well, aren't you so smart?" Pap snarled, crouching down to my level. "Reading like that just to show that you're better than your Pap. I'll find a way to bring you down a peg or two. Who told you to meddle in this schoolboy foolishness?"

My nose twitched. I couldn't miss the powerful scent of cheap whiskey coming from Pap's mouth.

"Pap, I ain't smart," I said, creeping backwards. "Honest, I'm not."

Pap grabbed me real rough by the fur of my neck. "Say, you know what I heard? I heard that you've become rich, boy. I heard that you found a heap of money in a cave and Judge Thatcher is keeping it for you."

I realized why Pap had suddenly grown so interested in me. He just wanted to get his hands on my money.

"Yes sir, I've got some money," I told Pap. "But the judge says I've got to leave it in the bank until I'm grown up. Please don't grab me so tight. You're hurting me!"

Pap let go of my fur, but he kept his eyes fixed on me. "You got any money on you now? If so, give it to me quick."

I fished a coin out of my pocket and set it on the floor.

"That's more like it," Pap said, snatching the coin. "I'll go buy myself a jug of whiskey. But don't get too comfortable here, Huck, because I'm coming back for you. And your money!"

Pap climbed out the window and left. But I knew I hadn't seen the last of him.

The next day, Pap went to Judge Thatcher, saying he wanted me to live with him and he wanted all my money too. Pap had the law on his side because, after all, he was my father. But Judge Thatcher didn't want to give me over to Pap. So he and Widow Douglas went to the courts, trying to get one of them made my legal guardian. Courts always take a long time with this sort of thing. They declared that I could stay with the Widow Douglas until a decision had been made.

I guess Pap got impatient waiting. One day when spring came around, he sprang out of nowhere and grabbed hold of my furred ear. He dragged me into a boat and we rowed about three miles down the river, docking on the Illinois shore. Pap had a log shanty, or shack, tucked back where the trees were so thick nobody could ever find it.

So then I was forced to live with my Pap. I didn't have to go to school no more and I was able to let my clothes get more raggedy and comfortable. But I had to deal with things that were even worse than spelling-books and starched collars.

Pap was always drunk and always in a bad mood. He cussed and yelled and beat me with a hickory stick. He went away a lot, off drinking and stealing things and what not, but those times weren't any better. He left me locked inside that miserable shanty, sometimes for several days. I didn't bother to escape, though. Pap would just come find me, I knew, and then he'd make things even harder on me. So I just kept on being a prisoner, licking my wounds and whimpering myself to sleep.

Oh, it got awful lonesome in that shanty.

One hazy summer day, Pap came home drunker than usual. He was covered with so much mud, he looked like a monster.

"They call this a government?" Pap yelled, stumbling around. "I hate this country's government! I hired a lawyer and he says I'll probably win the right to keep my son but he doesn't know how long it will take! I have a natural right to my son! But the courts keep dragging their feet!" He kicked a barrel. "Owww!"

Pap had hurt his foot, but he kept on hollering.

"I am your father! I go to all the trouble and worry and expense of raising you! Then just when you're grown and old enough to do something for me, they say they don't know if I can have you or not! Well, I tell you this, I will keep you locked away until they give me that money! And I'll take that money no matter what the court says!"

Then Pap picked up a jug of whiskey, which he tilted to his lips. As he guzzled, the liquor dribbled down his chin and muddy clothes. He got so busy drinking, he forgot I was even there. When darkness fell, Pap was still drinking away. So I curled up in the corner and went to sleep.

A bit later, my ears twitched, hearing a nightmarelike scream. I looked up from my spot on the floor. Pap was skipping about the room with a wild look in his eyes.

"Snakes! Snakes!" Pap cried, his voice choked with terror. "There's snakes all over me! They're crawling up my legs! They're wrapping around my face! Owww! One just bit me on the cheek! Get these snakes off of me!"

"There's no snakes on you!" I called to Pap. "You're just imagining it because you're so drunk!"

But Pap didn't hear me. He fell to the dirt floor, rolling over and over, kicking his legs, shaking his arms. Soon Pap's yelling gave way to crying. Then, worn out, he lay still.

Suddenly the shanty became quiet as a grave. Way off in the woods, I heard the mournful moan of an owl and a wolf howling to the moon. My fur felt all prickly from nervousness. I kept my eyes on Pap, wondering what he would do next.

Time dragged by. I'm not sure how much. Then Pap lifted his head, slow and careful. He seemed to be listening for something.

"Tramp, tramp, tramp," Pap whispered in an awfully weird voice. "I hear the footsteps of the dead. Yep, they're coming after me. I can feel the room getting colder."

Pap was acting so crazy, I didn't know what to do. Then he fixed his eyes on me and just stared for the longest time. But I got the feeling he wasn't really seeing me. He was seeing something else in my place. It was so scary, I felt my tail creeping between my legs.

"I know who you are," Pap finally whispered. "You're the Angel of Death. You're coming to take me away, aren't you?"

"I'm not the Angel of Death," I told Pap. "It's just me, your boy, Huck."

Don't lie!" Pap screamed, jumping to his feet. "I know you're the Angel of Death!"

Pap grabbed a sharp knife in his hand.

"I swear I'm no angel," I said, my four paws creeping backwards. "Just ask Widow Douglas or Miss Watson or Tom Sawyer or anyone else!"

With a yell, Pap leaped forward and swung the knife down at me. I jerked out of the way, just in time.

"I'll teach you to come after me with your fancy airs!" Pap hollered, waving the knife above his head. "I mean to get you before you can get me!"

"But Pap—"

Down the knife came, straight for my muzzle. I swerved away, feeling the blade whizz by, only an inch from my nose.

"I'll kill you right here and now!" Pap yelled in rage. "That way you won't be able to come after me ever again!"

Pap gave a screechy laugh that made my fur stick straight up. Then he chased me round and round the room, doing his best to slice me in half like a sausage. No matter how much I yipped or yelped or pleaded, I couldn't get him to stop coming after me with that knife. I was trapped and panting and scared out of my wits, but he just kept coming. Finally, he grabbed me and dragged me toward him. His eyes burning with evil, Pap pulled back the knife, preparing to plunge it into my chest.

I had to stop him. I jerked away from Pap and he let me go.I ran circles around him. He stumbled backwards, bumping into the wall, then crashing into a chair. My furred body trembled with a fear I'd never felt before or since.

Pap sank to the floor, exhausted, mumbling, "I just need to rest a minute. But after I do, I swear . . ."

Fortunately Pap fell into a stone-deep sleep. I could see that he wouldn't be bothering me anymore that night.

I lay down and rested my muzzle on my front paws. I realized that I had to get myself away from Pap or, sooner or later, he would kill me. The only question was . . . how could I escape?

The next morning, while I was checking my fishing lines by the river, I saw a canoe go drifting by. It was empty. I dog-paddled out to the canoe, then rowed it ashore. I hid it under some hanging willows.

A plan was coming to me.

That night when Pap went away to go to town and locked me in, I got to work. I've always had a special talent for digging. So I set my front paws in motion, digging at the shanty's dirt floor like there was no tomorrow. Pretty soon I had a tunnel big enough to let me crawl outside.

Making lots of trips, I carried all sorts of supplies to the canoe—bacon, coffee, sugar, fishing lines, a skillet, blankets, and several other things. I wanted to take the ax that Pap kept by the woodpile, but I had another use for it.

Grabbing the ax, I smashed the shanty's door, over and over again. The idea was to make it seem like a robber had broken in. There was dead pig lying outside that Pap had shot the day before. I dragged that big ol' pig through the broken door. Then I gave it a slice with a knife, letting the pig bleed all over the dirt. I rolled the ax blade in the blood. Then I used my teeth to pull a clump of fur off my chest and I stuck that fur on the bloody ax blade. Finally, I dragged the pig down to the river and sank it in the water.

My plan was done. Pap would think that a robber had broken into the shack, stole the supplies, and killed me. The trail made by the dragged pig would make it seem like the robber had dragged my body to the river and dumped it in. Pap and everyone else would believe that Huckleberry Finn was gone forever.

By then it was dark, and the moon was rising bright in the sky. I jumped into the canoe, then pushed off from shore. Gripping the paddle, I rowed my way down river about five miles.

Finally I saw the dark shape of Jackson's Island. I knew the island pretty well and knew that no one ever went there. Yep, that was the place for me.

I rowed myself to the shore. Then I tied the canoe to a willow tree, making sure that the drooping branches hid it from view. By this time, a touch of dawn showed in the sky. Dog-tired, I lay down for a good snooze.

Chapter Three

The midday sun woke me up.

I lay in the cool grass, resting my muzzle on my front paws. Sunshine drifted through the treetops, casting pretty freckled patterns on the ground.

Jackson's Island was small, and there weren't any people living there. It was mostly thick forest, dripping with old trees and wandering vines. This time of year, there were plenty of ripe berries and grapes growing. And there was no shortage of squirrels, rabbits, snakes, bugs, and bothersome mosquitoes.

I chewed on a stick, wondering what kind of food I was in the mood for.

Suddenly I heard a big loud BOOM!

I covered my ears. Then came several more deafening booms. I peeked through the leaves and saw a cloud of smoke hanging over the river. Nearby was a ferryboat full of people.

I realized what was happening. You see, whenever they wanted to find a dead body in the river, they would shoot a cannon over the water. The vibrations from the cannon would sometimes make the dead body float to the top. They were trying to find *my body!*

My tail wagged with relief. The plan had worked. The townsfolk really thought I was dead. Never again would I have to worry about the Widow Douglas or Miss Watson civilizing me. And I'd seen the last of Pap Finn and his hickory stick.

After a few hours, the people on the boat gave up on finding my body and went away. Then I made a tent from the blankets I had brought and built a cozy campfire. It was time for some vittles.

Two of my favorite things in life are chasing after cats and fishing for catfish. There weren't any cats on the island, but there were plenty of catfish swimming in the river. I threw out a few fishing lines. In no time at all, I pulled in a couple of real fine-looking catfish. I cleaned the fish, cut them into pieces, then fried them up in my skillet.

That's another one of my favorite things in life — eating.

Mmmm, boy, let me tell you, there's nothing quite like sinking your teeth into a piece of freshly fried catfish. When I was living with the Widow Douglas, I couldn't eat my supper until a supper bell rang. But out there in the wild, I was free to eat anytime or anywhere or anything I pleased.

After supper, I counted the stars, did some digging, caught up on some scratching, and listened to the river swish along the shore. Then I drifted off to sleep, feeling pretty well satisfied. I was boss of the whole island.

Three quiet days and three nights went by. Though I was glad to be on my own, I was beginning to feel lonesome. Then one afternoon, as I was chasing after sticks, I saw smoke drifting upwards at the tip of the island. My fur bristled with concern. It was a campfire. But whose?

I waited for night to fall. Then I moved through the shadowy woods until I had come to the island's tip. Through some trees, I saw the flickering of the campfire. I crept closer, keeping my body real low to the ground.

In a spill of moonlight, I saw a man stretched on the ground, fast asleep. But his head was covered by a blanket. I waited behind a clump of bushes, not moving a muscle. After a while, the moon disappeared and sunlight streaked the sky.

Soon the sleeping man stretched and tossed the blanket off his head. When I saw the man's face, my lower muzzle dropped with surprise. It was the slave owned by Miss Watson — Jim.

Time out for a history flash. As you probably know, there used to be slaves in this country. Large groups of black men, women, and children were captured in Africa and brought to North America in ships. They were forced to work for no pay and they had no real rights. They were treated

like property, not people.

The slaves were especially important in the South, where the economy depended on the free labor of the slaves in the cotton fields and farms. Back in Huck Finn's time, slavery wasn't considered a bad thing in the South. Many people thought that owning slaves was as natural as owning horses or cattle.

Okay, Huck, back to you.

Jim was a big black fellow with a friendly way about him. I trusted Jim would never hurt me, even though his arms were plenty muscular from all the hard farm work he did.

"Hello, Jim," I said, coming out from my hiding place.

Jim stared at me like I was a ghost.

"Don't hurt me!" he cried, suddenly falling to his knees and putting his hands together. "I never did nothing to harm a dead person! Matter of fact, I like dead people. You just go on back into that river, Mr. Huck, where you belong!"

I realized that he thought I really *was* a ghost. I fixed that right away by telling him how I was only pretending to be dead so as to escape from my Pap.

"How long have you been on this island?" Jim asked, growing calmer.

"Since the night I was killed," I said. "How about you?"

"Since the night *after* you were killed."

"How did you get to be here?"

Jim looked uneasy. "Mr. Huck, you wouldn't tell on me, would you?"

"No, I wouldn't. And you can just drop that 'mister' from my name. You don't need to show me any respect."

"I ran away, Huck."

This worried me a bit. I happened to like most of the slaves I knew. But even so, I knew it was downright illegal for a slave to run away from his or her rightful owner.

"Why did you run away?" I asked.

Jim took a seat on the grass, looking real solemn. "I overheard Miss Watson talking to the Widow Douglas one night. Miss Watson said she was planning to sell me to a slave trader for eight hundred dollars. Well, that was bad news for me. I knew the slave trader would take me down to New Orleans and sell me at a slave auction. Then there's no telling where I'd end up. I might never see my wife and children again. So I . . . I run away."

"Well, I guess you did what you had to do," I said quietly.

Jim nodded then said, "Say, I'm starving, Huck. How about we get ourselves something to eat?"

"Jim," I said, giving him a playful swipe with my paw, "now you're talking my language!"

Ten or twelve days went by without much happening. Jim and I explored, hunted, fished, ate, slept, talked, and had what you might call an all-around relaxing time.

All sorts of interesting things were always floating by on the river. One night, Jim and I caught hold of a raft, the type used for hauling things. It was a good-size raft made from pine-wood planks. Jim said we should keep the raft, as we might have some use for it later on.

Another time, we rowed my canoe out to a houseboat that went floating by. There didn't seem to be any passengers aboard. Jim stole a look in the house window to see what might be inside.

"Anything interesting in there?" I said, rising to my hind legs. "Like, for example, some steaks or frankfurters?"

Jim looked down at me, his face real serious. "There's a dead man in there, Huck. Looks like he's been shot in the back."

"Pick me up, Jim, so I can have a look."

"Nah, I don't want you looking at that man. It's too frightening a sight."

Jim went inside the house part of the boat and threw a blanket over the dead body. Then Jim and I snooped around, looking for useful supplies. We found all sorts of things—a tin lantern, candles, a hunting knife, a hatchet, some nails, empty whiskey bottles, clothing for men and women, plenty of books, a fiddle bow, and a horseshoe. Oh yeah, I also found an old straw hat that I instantly took a fancy to. Jim and I loaded the supplies in our canoe, then let the boat go drifting down river.

Later that night, Jim and I were relaxing by our campfire. We had just finished a hearty dinner.

"Jim," I said, "why do you suppose that man on the houseboat was killed?"

"Let's not talk about it," Jim advised. "Talking about a dead person is a good way to bring bad luck."

"Hmmm, I didn't know that. Tell me some other things that bring bad luck. Then I'll know not to do them."

"Don't ever shake a tablecloth after sundown," Jim said. "Don't ever look at a new moon over your left shoulder. And don't ever, ever, ever touch a snakeskin with your bare hands. That's about the worst thing you can do."

I rested my muzzle on a log. "You know all kinds of things, don't you, Jim?"

"I reckon so," Jim said, gazing upward. "See those young birds yonder? After they fly a few yards, they stop and perch in the trees. That means a rain'll be coming in the next few days. So we better be looking for a nice cave to shelter ourselves."

"Are there any signs for good luck?" I asked eagerly.

"Nah, not really. But I do know this. If a person's got a hairy chest, that means that person is going to get rich."

"Hey, I might end up a millionaire."

"Come to think of it," Jim said, a little sadly, "I wish I knew a few ways to bring on some good luck. Ol' Jim hasn't seen too much of that lately."

"Maybe rubbing the top of my head will bring you good luck," I suggested. "Kind of like rubbing a tin lamp to summon a genie."

"I'll give it a try," Jim said, showing a friendly smile.

Jim rubbed the top of my head and looked around. "Now where's that genie?" I was glad to have Jim around. I didn't have to be lonesome no more.

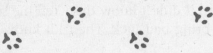

As more days rolled by, I found myself getting restless for some new activity or even some new news. I decided to pay a brief visit back to St. Petersburg. Jim said that would be all right as long as I went in disguise.

I dressed myself as a girl, using a calico dress and sun-bonnet that we'd brought from the houseboat. All afternoon, I practiced walking and talking in a dainty way. Tom Sawyer would have been proud of me for the pretty job of pretending I was doing.

As night fell, I rowed the canoe across the river and tied it up just below town. Near the shore, I found a log cabin that I had never visited before. When I scratched at the door, a lady opened up and very politely invited me inside.

"What might your name be?" the lady said as I took a seat on the floor.

"Sarah Williams," I said, trying to make my voice sound as girly as my dress and sun-bonnet. "I walked here all the way from my hometown of Hookerville."

She knelt down to me. "Why don't you take off your bonnet?"

"Oh, no," I said, pulling my head back. "I don't like to take off my bonnet. That's because . . . I have big ears. I'll just rest awhile, then be on my way."

The lady sat in a rocking chair and talked to me. Among other things, she told me about a boy named Huckleberry Finn who had recently been murdered in town.

"Do they know who done it?" I asked.

"At first, everyone thought it was his pap," the lady replied. "But then everyone started thinking that the crime was done by a runaway slave named Jim."

I lifted a paw to protest but then thought better of it.

"You see," the lady continued, "the slave ran off the night after Huck Finn was killed. Right now there's a reward out for this slave. Three hundred dollars for anyone who can find him. It shouldn't take too long."

"Why do you say that?"

"Because a lot of folks would like the reward money. Besides, I think the slave is just yonder on Jackson's Island. I saw campfire smoke over there the other day. My husband's going out to the island to search for him."

"When?" I asked, lifting my ears a bit.

"Tonight. He and another man are out right now hiring a boat and borrowing an extra gun. They should be leaving around midnight."

My tail jumped at the news. Fortunately this sign of panic was covered by my long dress.

The lady looked at me real close. "What did you say your name was again?"

"Uh . . . Mary Williams."

"Honey, I thought you said it was Sarah."

"Well . . . it is. Sarah . . . Mary . . . Williams."

"Oh, dear," the lady said, glancing at the corner. "I see another rat. Would you help me scare it away?"

I was glad to help out. Going to the corner, I gave a ferocious growl.

"That ought to do the trick," I said proudly.

The lady gave me a funny smile. "No girl goes after a rat like that. Why don't you tell me what your *real* name is. Is it Billy or Bob or George or what?"

I lowered my muzzle and pretended to whimper. I was just stalling so I could think up something to say.

The lady came over and stroked my back. "There, there, you have nothing to fear. I don't mean you any harm. I just want to know who you really are."

So I told her a fib about how I was running away in disguise from the mean ol' farmer I lived with. I said I was searching for my Uncle Abner in the town of Goshen. When she mentioned that Goshen was ten

40

miles upriver, I said, well, I better get going then. That last statement was true.

The lady opened the door for me. "So long, Sarah-Mary-Billy-Bob-George or whoever you are. Good luck finding your uncle."

The second I left the cabin, I ran my fastest. It wasn't easy, though, because my paws kept tripping over the hem of my dress. Soon I jumped in the canoe and rowed in a hurry for the tip of Jackson's Island.

I scampered to the campsite, where Jim was sleeping. After tearing my bonnet off, I pawed at Jim's arm. When he opened his eyes, I cried, "Jim, get yourself up! There ain't a minute to lose! They're after us!"

Jim didn't ask no questions but I could see that he was plenty scared. Jim and I, we put out the campfire, then piled all of our supplies onto that wooden raft we had found. Then we tied the canoe to the raft with a rope. Without saying a single word, we shoved off from the shore and steered our raft into the mighty Mississippi River.

Whew, Huck and Jim escape in the nick of time. Hey, I've got some escaping of my own to do.

Chapter Four

After escaping the Talbot house, Wishbone raced through the backyard, He stopped just short of the neighboring Barnes house. Seeing someone, he ducked behind a shrub.

I can't let anyone see me, the dog thought with concern. *They might tell Ellen where I am, and before I know it . . . I'll be a dog in a dress!*

Mrs. Barnes stood by the car in her driveway.

"Emily," she called toward the house. "If we don't leave now, we'll be late for the carnival!"

Wishbone noticed that the door to the Barnes house was open. When Mrs. Barnes climbed into the car, Wishbone made a break for the house. He slipped through the front door and hid behind an umbrella-stand. He watched as five-year-old Emily Barnes tramped down the stairs and out the door.

So far, so good, Wishbone thought as the door shut behind her. *Hey, I can hide out in David's room for a while. He won't give me away.*

Wishbone ran up the steps and trotted into one of his homes away from home—David Barnes's bedroom, which looked like a tornado had hit it. Clothes, books, papers, and electronic equipment were scattered everywhere.

"It's got to be here . . . somewhere," David muttered, rifling through the top drawer of his dresser. The same age as Joe, David had curly, black hair and intense eyes that never missed a trick. He was a whiz-kid with computers or anything else mechanical. He was also a totally trusted friend of Joe's.

"David, what happened?" Wishbone asked, stepping over a strong-smelling sneaker. "It looks like a tornado hit."

David was too busy to answer.

Wishbone took a seat, watching David go through his dresser drawers, one by one. When David got to the bottom, drawer, Wishbone heard the front door open downstairs.

"David, are you home?" a voice called.

Wishbone recognized the voice of Samantha Kepler.

"Yeah, I'm upstairs," David called without looking up.

"I'm on my way over to Joe's," Sam called. "Are you busy?"

"Come on up," David called.

"David, listen up," Wishbone whispered. "I don't want Sam to know that I'm here because she might tell Joe, and Joe might tell Ellen. And Ellen wants to make me wear some clothes from the Canine Couture collection. It's a long story, okay? Just pretend I'm not here and that we never had this conversation."

43

Although David was still searching through the drawer, Wishbone was pretty sure he got the message.

Wishbone hid under the bed just as Sam peered into the room. Twelve-year-old Sam warmed the room like a ray of sunshine. That was Sam—sunny, warm, and kind.

"David, what happened to your room?" Sam asked, tucking her long blonde hair over one shoulder. "Was there an earthquake that I didn't hear about?"

"I'm looking for something."

"Like what?" she asked.

David sighed. "It's a long story."

"I've got time," Sam said patiently.

David pushed a stack of CDs aside and slumped down to the floor. From under the bed, Wishbone watched and listened.

"I've been hanging out with my friend Gilbert," David began, "He just got a Zip-T for his birthday, and I—"

"Hold on," Sam said, sitting cross-legged beside him. "What's a Zip-T?"

I was wondering the same thing, Wishbone thought.

"It's a T-shaped computer that's small enough to hold in your hand," David explained. "It's brand new—cutting-edge."

Sam shrugged. "Sounds cool, I guess."

"It's super cool," David said. "It's also super expensive. As in, four hundred dollars. But Gilbert's parents went for it because it was his birthday."

"Go on," Sam said.

"So I was playing this game on the Zip-T," David continued. "And Gilbert said I could borrow it for a few days. So I took it home with me."

"And you lost it?" Sam asked, wincing.

David nodded. "I've been looking for twenty minutes. I just can't think where it could be."

Oh, I hate it when I lose something valuable, Wishbone thought. *One time, I lost this really nice chew-toy that—*

"When was the last time you saw it?" Sam asked.

"This morning. I took it to my friend Lisa's house. We played with it awhile. Then I put it back in my backpack and rode my bike home. That was about half an hour ago."

"Is there any chance you left it at Lisa's house?"

"No, I remember taking it out and putting it on my desk."

Sam glanced at the desk and shrugged. "So it must be here."

"But it's not, and I've searched everywhere. Oh, my dad was right." David rubbed his face. "I showed him the Zip-T and he didn't like the idea of me borrowing such an expensive device. If it got broken or lost, he said, I would be responsible. He thought I should take it back to Gilbert right away."

"But you didn't," Sam said.

David shook his head. "I was just going to keep it one more day. But you know me, Sam. I'm very careful with these things."

Very *careful,* Wishbone thought. *You treasure computer equipment the way I treasure bones.*

"Have you told Gilbert it's lost yet?" Sam asked.

"No. But he's coming to pick it up tonight."

"Have you told your dad?"

David buried his face in his hands. "Not yet. He'll probably ground me for a few weeks, maybe a few months. But I feel so bad about the whole thing, I'll probably ground *myself*."

I hate being grounded, Wishbone thought. *I'll never forget the time I was accidentally locked up in the dog pound for—*

"Let me help," Sam said sympathetically.

"No," David said. "It's definitely gone. Right now I just need to be alone. And please don't mention this to anyone."

"I won't say a word." Sam stood up. "And I'll check with you later."

"Thanks," David said as she left the room.

Wishbone crept out from under the bed. "Hey, nice job pretending I wasn't here."

David looked at Wishbone with surprise. "Wishbone, I didn't know you were here."

Wishbone nodded his muzzle. "That's the spirit."

"Where could that thing be?" David said, pounding a fist on the floor.

Wishbone tried to be helpful. "Whenever I get my

paws on something really valuable, like, say, an old sock, I like to bury it for safekeeping. Is there any chance you might have buried this computer somewhere?"

David didn't answer.

"Well, maybe not," Wishbone said, sitting beside David. "What a day. We're both in a tight situation. You're about to be grounded, and I'm about to lose my dignity. But we need to stick together. Tell you what. I'll help you deal with getting grounded and you help me deal with getting stuck in a pink tutu. Deal?"

"Wait a second." David sprang to his feet. "I've got an idea. Come on, Wishbone, let's take a walk!"

Wishbone padded along right beside him. "Sounds good to me. Matter of fact, maybe we should just keep walking until we're in the next county."

When your freedom is threatened, there's nothing like having a good friend to help out. I've got David on my side and Huck's got Jim. So . . while David and I head out for a walk, let's follow Huck and Jim down the river.

Chapter Five

In the dark of night, Jim and I rode our raft through the muddy waters of the Mississippi River. When those men came looking for Jim on Jackson's Island, they wouldn't find anything but the ashy remains of our campfire.

The Mississippi was an awfully big river in those parts, over a mile and half wide. The water lay around us, black as a Labrador retriever's fur. There were mostly mountains on the Missouri shore, and thick woods on the Illinois shore. Scattered about were lots of tiny sparks. They were the candles burning in the house windows.

Jim and I each had a long pole, which we used to steer the raft by dipping the poles in the water. We also used a wooden tiller, or steering device, that was attached to the back of the raft. The Mississippi was a tricky river to navigate. The currents were always shifting around, going fast then slow, pulling the raft this way and that.

The mighty Mississippi is the second longest river in the world, right behind the Amazon River in South America. It starts in St. Paul, Minnesota, and winds south to New Orleans, Louisiana. If you're counting, that's over two thousand miles.

Back in Huck Finn's time—before cars and trains and airplanes—traveling by boat on the rivers was the best way to move passengers and cargo. And the Mississippi was an especially busy waterway. It was filled with . . . well, why don't I let Huck tell you the rest?

Since it was night, there wasn't too much activity on the water. But during the day the Mississippi had more traffic than the main street of most towns. There were rafts and canoes and skiffs carrying coal, lumber, interesting people, and, well, practically anything you can imagine. Best of all were the steamboats.

Steamboats were like giant floating palaces, most of them painted white and decorated with all sorts of fancy designs. They each had two tall chimneys, which sent up swirls of black smoke, and an oversized paddle-wheel or two. Those steam-powered wheels rolled and rolled, churning the water into a milky white foam. Jim and I had to be real careful whenever a steamboat was coming our way because it could flatten us like a griddlecake.

When the first streak of dawn appeared, Jim and I tied the raft to the shore and covered it with a bunch of cut branches. Jim told me that runaway slaves always traveled by night and rested by day. That way they were less likely to get caught.

So Jim and I spent the day lazing in the grass and catching some sleep. With the sun soothing my fur and Jim right beside me, I felt totally safe and content. When night fell, we set off again. That became our routine—resting all day, traveling all night. All the while, we kept heading downriver, drifting in a southerly direction.

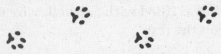

Jim and I had some mighty fine nights on that river. Usually we'd let the raft float along, going wherever the current wanted her to go. Sometimes we'd dangle our legs in the water or take a swim to keep off the sleepiness.

As we passed by towns, we'd see their lights twinkling on the hillsides. The fifth night we passed St. Louis, and it was like the whole world lit up. I had heard there were twenty or thirty thousand people in St. Louis, but I never believed it till I saw its wonderful spread of lights.

Most nights around ten o'clock, I'd slip ashore and buy some things for our food supply—cornmeal, bacon, watermelons, cantaloupes, and such. We also caught plenty of catfish to eat.

Have I mentioned yet how much I like catfish?

After midnight, the lights in all the houses along

the shore would go out. Sometimes it seemed like we had the whole river to ourselves. You can't imagine how quiet and still that river got real late at night. By then, millions of stars speckled the sky. Jim and I lay on the raft for hours admiring those stars.

One night I asked, "Jim, how do you reckon all those stars got to be there?"

"I reckon they must have been made by someone," Jim replied.

"Myself, I think they just happened to be there. It would have taken too long to make them. There's just so many."

After a moment's thought, Jim said, "Maybe they were laid by the moon."

"That's a good point," I said, nodding my muzzle. "I've seen frogs lay almost as many tadpoles. Yeah, maybe you're right."

With a low chuckle, Jim rubbed my head for good luck.

The fifth night below St. Louis, a big summer storm blew in. A wild wind blasted the passing trees, and the rain poured down in a solid sheet. The sky was pitch-black, but now and then—kazow—lightning filled the sky, bright as glory. And oh, how the thunder rumbled and grumbled like an empty barrel tumbling down a flight of stairs.

The storm didn't bother us, though. A few days earlier, Jim had built a kind of wigwam on the raft to protect us from bad weather. The wigwam was made from spare planks of wood, and the middle of the floor was covered with dirt. That allowed us to build a fire in there. As the storm raged, Jim and I kept dry and cozy inside. We even cooked ourselves a tasty supper.

"Ain't this nice?" Jim said, checking the skillet. "Just watching that rain pour down all around us."

"I wouldn't want to be nowhere else but here," I said, licking some fish grease off my paws. "Jim, pass me another hunk of fish and some hot cornbread."

"Coming right up," Jim said with a grin.

Yes sir, life was mighty free and easy on that raft.

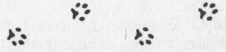

After traveling a few more nights, Jim and I figured we were nearing the town of Cairo, Illinois. At Cairo, the Ohio River runs into the Mississippi River. We planned to sell the raft in Cairo, then maybe earn some money doing odd jobs. Then we could buy tickets to a steamboat that would carry us up the Ohio River. This would take us into the northern states, where people weren't allowed to own slaves. This was very exciting for Jim.

"The minute we see Cairo," Jim said, flashing a smile, "I'll be on my way to freedom!"

"How will we know when we've hit Cairo?" I asked, looking across the black water. "I hear it's just a real small town. It might be easy to miss in the dark."

"The Ohio River is nice and clear. But the Mississippi River is all muddy," Jim explained. "If we was traveling by day, we could just keep an eye out for that clear water. But we'll be traveling by night. We'll just have to watch real sharp for the first sight of the Ohio River. I won't miss it though. Just thinking about my freedom makes me all filled with joy!"

But it made my whiskers twitch with worry. I'll tell you why.

When I left Jackson's Island with Jim, I just did it without thinking. I did it because I liked Jim and wanted his company. But even though I didn't come from a respectable family, I wasn't the kind of boy who goes breaking the law. But the truth is, I *was* breaking the law by helping Jim get away. He was a slave, and that meant he was really just a piece of property—a piece of property that belonged to Miss Watson.

I lay down, resting my muzzle on my front paws, thinking.

Pretty soon, it seemed like my conscience was talking to me. It seemed to whisper in my ear, *What has poor Miss Watson ever done to you? How could you let her slave get away and not say a single word? That lady tried to teach you right from wrong and all you do in return is treat her mean!*

Just then, Jim sat down beside me. "Huck, listen. You know what I'm going to do as soon as I'm free? I'll get myself a job and I'll save every single cent. And when I've got enough money, I'll buy my wife from her owner. She works on a farm not too far from Miss Watson. And then we'll both go to work and save enough money to buy our children. They work on a farm not too far away from my wife."

"What if the owners won't sell your wife and children to you?" I asked.

Jim thought a moment, then said, "I'll just have to steal them. One way or another, I'm going to live with my family."

I rose to all fours and walked away because it

seemed like my conscience was whispering to me again. It seemed to say, *You hear that? The slave is talking about stealing his wife and children. Stealing property that doesn't belong to him. Are you just going to stand by and let him do it?*

All right! I yelled at my conscience. *Let up on me! It ain't too late yet! I'll find a way out of this mess!*

I went back to Jim. "Uh, looky. Maybe I should go out in the canoe and see if I can get a glimpse of Cairo."

This was a lie, though. I was really planning to find some passersby in a boat and tell them that I was traveling with a runaway slave. That's right. I was planning to turn Jim in.

I jumped into the canoe we had brought with us, untied it, and rowed away from the raft.

"Pretty soon I'll be shouting for joy," Jim called out to me. "I'll be a free man. And it's all because of Huck Finn. He helped me get free. No sir, I won't ever forget you, Huck. You're the best friend ol' Jim ever had!"

When Jim said this, my ears drooped with guilty feelings. But I just kept telling myself, *Huck, you've got to obey your conscience. And your conscience wants you to obey the law.*

After rowing a ways, I saw a small boat that contained two men holding rifles. I rowed the canoe alongside of them.

"Did you come from that raft?" one of the men asked me.

"Yes, sir," I answered.

"Any men on the raft?" the man asked.

"Only one, sir," I said.

Then the other man spoke, running a finger along the barrel of his rifle. "Well, five slaves ran away tonight just above the bend. We're out looking for them. We plan to haul them back in. Of course, we'll take any other runaway slaves we find, too. Is your man white or black?"

I started to say that my man was black, but somehow the words got stuck in my throat. I tried again, but this time the words came out different.

I said, "The man on my raft is white."

"I reckon we better go see for ourselves." the first man said, giving me a suspicious eye.

My tail thumped the canoe nervously. I knew I needed to come up with a good white lie or those men would go to the raft and find that Jim was black.

"I wish you would go see that man on the raft because he's my pap," I told the men. "He's sick. So is my mama and my sister. They're all sick. Maybe you could help me tow the raft to shore."

Both men looked disappointed by this news

"We're busy looking for runaway slaves," the first man grumbled. "But I suppose we ought to help."

"Oh, thank you so much," I said. "Everyone goes away when I ask for help. That's because, well . . . my family's got smallpox."

"Smallpox!" one man gasped.

"We got to be going!" the other man exclaimed.

Those two men rowed away from me faster than a raccoon with a fire on its tail. Smallpox was a disease, worse than ringworm or fleas or any other kind of illness a person might catch. I guess I just didn't have the heart to turn Jim in.

As I rowed back to the raft, I seemed to hear my conscience again. It told me, *You ain't never going to learn to do right, Huckleberry Finn. You're going to end up in that bad place deep underground where it's hot all the time.*

Looky! I told my conscience. *Suppose I had done right and turned Jim in. Would I feel better? No, I'd feel even worse. What's the use of learning to do the right thing when it's just going to make you feel worse than when you do the wrong thing?*

My conscience couldn't figure out a good answer for that. So it quit arguing with me . . . at least for the time being.

The very next night, we expected to reach Cairo. We watched extra sharp because a smoky fog had settled over the river. But we figured our calculations must have been off because there was no sign of Cairo.

When dawn came, we tied the raft along the shore. In the growing light, I noticed some clear water mixing with the Mississippi's muddy-brown water.

"Jim," I said, giving him a gentle nudge with my muzzle. "Take a look at that clear water."

One glance at the water and Jim realized what had happened.

"Oh, Lordy." He sank onto a rock. "That clear water means we missed the turn-off into the Ohio River. We must've plain missed Cairo in the fog. Oh, there's no luck anywhere for poor Jim."

We had to get some sleep, so we lay down in the shade of some trees. When we woke up, things got even worse. Our canoe was gone. The rope tying it to the raft had come loose and then the current had carried it away.

The only way to get back to Cairo, which was upriver, was in a canoe or steamboat. But our canoe was gone, and we didn't have enough money to buy steamboat tickets. You see, the raft wasn't able to work its way against the river's strong current. This meant we had to keep on heading downriver, farther south— deeper into slave country.

After dark, we shoved out on the raft. The fog was thick, like a smoky white ghost hovering over the river. It gave me the creeps. After a while I noticed something that looked like a black mountain surrounded by glowworms.

My tail flicked with alarm. "Jim, it's a steamboat! It's coming straight our way! "

"Stop!" Jim yelled at the steamboat, waving our lantern in the air. "Stop! Don't hit us! Stop! Please, stop!"

Soon I heard the powerful sound of the steam engine pounding louder and louder. It felt like someone was beating a drum inside my ears. The raft began shaking beneath my paws. The glowworm lights on the boat grew brighter and brighter, like tiny suns. Either the steamboat didn't see us or it was too late for that giant vehicle to slow itself down.

"They're about to hit us!" Jim shouted. "Jump, Huck!"

Just as Jim and I both leaped overboard, the steamboat crashed smack into our raft.

Paddling madly with my paws, I pulled myself deeper and deeper underwater. I knew I needed to steer clear of that steamboat's big wheel or else I'd be a dead dog. Finally, I had to breathe so bad I felt as if I'd pop out of my fur. Up to the surface I shot, panting and gasping for air.

The steamboat kept moving through the river, disappearing into the ghostly fog.

"Jim!" I barked out. "Where are you? Jim! Jim!"

The river was all silence.

"Jim! You can't be gone! I need you! Where are you?"

Still, there was no reply. It seemed that Jim must have been killed by that steamboat wheel. With a terrible pain tugging at my heart, I dog-paddled all the way to shore.

Exhausted and drenched, I staggered onto land and gave my fur a few good shakes. Even after I dried off, I was still shivering head to tail. Once again, Huck Finn was all alone in the world.

Chapter Six

The night was so doggone dark, my eyes weren't much help. So I put my trusty nose to the ground and found my way to a big porch lined with a row of white columns. It was a mansion, grand as a king's castle. Raising my front paw, I gave the front door a scratch.

The door opened, and a black butler-slave stood there, looking curiously down at me.

A kindly family called the Grangerfords lived in that mansion. When I told them I was just a penniless orphan, they invited me in. They said I could stay as long as I liked. Not having anywhere else to go, I accepted the offer.

The Grangerfords were what you call "aristocrats" —a rich family that owned a vast cotton plantation and over a hundred black slaves. Colonel Grangerford, the head of the family, always wore a white suit that shone so brightly it almost hurt your eyes.

The eating was mighty fine at that place. Every

66

6666666

66

night was a feast—ham steak, pork chops, fried chicken, greens, corn, grits with butter, biscuits with gravy, cobbler, and every kind of pie in the world. Mmmm, I'm licking my chops just thinking about it.

But there was one thing I didn't like about the Grangerfords. For the past thirty years or so, they had been feuding with the Shepherdsons, another aristocratic family in the area. No one could remember why the feud began, but those two families were determined to kill each other off. The Grangerfords and the Shepherdsons took their guns everywhere, even to church. Both sides were always looking for the other to start something up. It made me feel like I was caught between two hissing cats.

After several weeks at the Grangerford place, one of the family slaves took me down to a swamp near the river. Imagine my surprise when I saw Jim standing there.

"Jim!" I cried, wagging my tail with sudden joy. "By jings, Jim, I'm so awfully glad you're alive!"

With a big smile, Jim swooped me up into the air. "And I'm glad to see you, Huck! After we jumped off the raft, the current must have pulled us a long way apart. I looked all over but I couldn't find you. My heart was almost broke, thinking you might be dead. Then, about a week ago, I met one of the Grangerford slaves and learned you were staying with the family."

"Why didn't you send for me then?"

"I didn't want to pull you away from all that good food until I was ready."

"Ready for what?" I asked.

"I found the raft and patched it up," Jim ex-

plained. "It's better than ever now. I've been gathering supplies too. We're ready to sail off any time now."

"Then let's get going," I said. "I like the food around here but not the feuding. I'd be pleased to leave tonight!"

And so when darkness fell, Jim and I rode down the river on our very own raft. I felt like I had returned to my true home.

Two or three days slid quietly by, and our raft crossed into the state of Arkansas. The nights on the river were wonderful, but in a way, the daytimes were almost as nice.

While it was still dark, Jim and I would hide the raft somewhere along the shore. Then we'd take a brief dip in the water to cool off. Then we'd sit in a shallow part of the water to watch the daylight come.

At those times, it seemed like the whole world was asleep. There wouldn't be a single sound, except maybe for a bullfrog uttering his peculiar sound. Soon a paleness would spread across the sky, magically turning the water from black to gray. A mist would rise up from the river, and we'd start to see rafts and boats drifting on their daily journey. Before long, the sun would be smiling in the east, and the songbirds would be singing their hearts out.

Then Jim and I would cook up a hot breakfast. After that, we'd laze around awhile before drifting into a peaceful sleep. Jim liked to lie on his back, a blanket covering his face. Myself, I preferred to curl up into a furry ball.

Soon as darkness came again, Jim and I would shove off for another night of traveling.

Jim and I had found a bunch of books on that dead man's houseboat. Some nights, I would read to Jim by the light of our lantern. The books were mostly about kings and dukes and earls and such.

"What exactly does a king do?" Jim asked me one night.

"They don't do nothing," I said. "They just sit around being kings. We don't have any kings in this country, though."

"None?"

"Well, there might be one," I said, scratching my side as I remembered a history lesson from school. "Louis the Sixteenth, the last king of France, got his head cut off a while back. His son was thrown in jail, but some folks say that he escaped and came to this country. He's called the dauphin."

"Why is he a dolphin? I thought they were in the sea."

"Not dolphin. I said *dauphin*. I think it's the French word for "prince.""

Jim was plenty smart, and there's no way I could have got by so well without him. He just didn't know about certain things because he had never been to school.

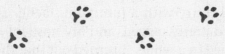

Now, you'll never believe what happened a few mornings later.

I was snooping through some trees near a town, sniffing for fresh berries. My ears shot up as footsteps pounded across the ground. Suddenly two men appeared in my path. They were huffing and puffing and hauling big bags made from carpet material.

"Hey, you!" one of the fellows whispered to me. "You've got to help us! I assure you that we are innocent of any crime, but—

"But they're chasing after us!" the other fellow picked up. "And they've got hound dogs!"

Sure enough, I heard the footsteps of approaching men and the sharp barks of hound dogs. The two fellows looked so scared and panicky I felt sorry for them. I also knew something about the way hound dogs worked.

"Here's what you do," I told the men. "Don't run

across the land. Wade through the water. That way the dogs won't be able to pick up on your scent. Head for the southern shore. You'll find a raft hidden by some branches. I'll be there waiting for you."

A few minutes later, I met the two men by the raft. My plan had worked because I could hear that the men and dogs were taking their hunt in the opposite direction. Jim and I eyed the strangers, wondering who they might be.

The first fellow was about seventy years old with a bald head and a scraggly gray beard. The other fellow was around thirty with a funny mustache. They were both dressed pretty ragged, and my nose told me they hadn't bathed in a while. It turned out that the two fellows didn't know each other. They only met because they were both being chased out of the same town at the same time.

"What got you in trouble?" the older fellow asked the younger.

"I was selling a paste that cleans the tartar off of teeth," the younger fellow explained. "And it *does* take it off. Problem is, it takes most of the tooth with it. And you?"

"I gave dancing lessons," the older fellow replied. "But the customers discovered that I don't know how to dance any better than a jackrabbit. So they danced me out of town."

I tilted my head. These sounded like awfully odd jobs to me. Jim looked confused too.

The younger man gave a woeful sigh. "Alas, to fall from so high to so low so quickly. Look at what I have become. Alas, to suffer such misfortune."

"What are you talking about?" I asked.

"Gentlemen," the young fellow said. "I will reveal the secret of my birth. I am the duke of Bridgewater, forced to flee my native country for political purposes. Imagine, a royal person like me forced to live the life of a poor wanderer."

I'd never heard of a country called Bridgewater. But then I was never too good at geography in school.

Jim looked at the duke with curiosity. "Forgive me, sir, but I'm not sure how to act around a duke."

"Oh, there's not much to it," the duke said with a casual gesture. "Just bow to me frequently, wait on me at meals, and address me as 'Your Highness.'"

Jim and I nodded thoughtfully. But the old fellow was stroking his beard, looking sort of jealous.

Finally he said, "Listen here, Bilgewater—"

"The name is Bridgewater," the duke pointed out.

"Whatever you're called," the old fellow said, "you're not the only royalty around here."

"He's not?" Jim and I said together.

The old fellow placed a hand on his heart. "I am, in truth, the dauphin of France. By all rights, I should be the king of France by now, but ever since the revolution, my people have refused to let me back in the country. However, the three of you may call me 'Your Majesty.'"

My ears seemed to jump a mile high, and Jim's eyes almost bugged out of his head. The duke, on the other hand, looked jealous that he had been outranked by a king.

"Do you speak French?" Jim asked the king of France.

"Uhm, well, of course," the king said, after clearing his throat. "But you see, I'm so used to speaking English now that I don't remember my French very well."

The duke turned a suspicious eye on Jim. "Say, you wouldn't be a runaway slave, would you?"

"Of course, he's not a runaway slave," I said. "Why would a slave be running south instead of north? No, he belongs to my pap but . . . my pap he drowned recently so, uh . . . Jim and I are going to live with . . . my great-grandfather in New Orleans. We don't travel in the daytime, though, because a lot of folks *think* Jim is a runaway slave."

Thankfully, the duke and king seemed to buy my fib.

When darkness fell, the four of us rode the raft down the river. Soon a storm blew through, hammering us with rain and roughness. My fur got drenched that night because Jim and I let the duke and king have the wigwam. It seemed like the proper thing to do.

Over the next few days, the king and duke played cards and discussed how they might team up to make some money. I came to realize that neither of them was real royalty. No sir, those two were just a pair of scoundrels, fellows who lie and cheat to make an easy buck. I didn't say anything, though. Sometimes it's best just to keep peace in the pack.

Finally the duke had an idea. "Your Majesty, I know what we'll do. We'll put on a Shakespearean performance!"

"Your Highness," the king said, "I'm all for anything that pays the rent. But I confess, I don't know much about play acting."

"I'll teach you everything," the duke said, springing dramatically to his feet. "The first act will be the balcony scene from *Romeo and Juliet*. The second act will be the sword fight from *Richard the Third*. I'll play Romeo and Richard, you'll play Juliet and Richmond."

The duke pulled out some costumes from his carpetbag, and the two fellows began rehearsing. Furry as I was, I believe I would have made a better Juliet than the king. Juliet was supposed to be a young girl, but the king was a big, bearded, bald-headed old man. The duke bellowed his lines like a wounded cow, and the king brayed his lines like a sick donkey.

The sword fight didn't go much better. The duke and king pranced around the raft, clanging swords with each other. I kept dancing out of the way to keep my paws from getting trampled. Several times, the king toppled overboard into the water. Poor Jim didn't know what to make of any of this.

A few days later, we stopped in a little one-horse town called Brickville. The streets were mostly mud, but that didn't stop the hogs from roaming around, searching for scraps of food. The king and duke rented the courthouse for their performance. I spent the afternoon helping them set up a stage and curtain and candle footlights. Then I wandered around town, examining various trees and trying to drum up business for the show. Most of the folks didn't seem too interested in Shakespeare, though. Neither did the hogs.

That night, only about a dozen people showed up for the performance. The acting was so loud and bad, I slipped under my chair and covered my ears with my paws. The rest of the audience left early, except for a small boy who was snoring by the end.

"We need to draw a bigger audience somehow," the king grumbled after the show.

"I know just the thing," the duke said with a snap of his fingers. "No more Shakespeare. What these folks want is something really exciting!"

The next day, the duke painted up a bunch of handbills, which we posted all over the town. The handbills announced:

At the Court House! For 3 nights only!
David Garrick, the Younger, and
Edmund Kean, Elder,
Present their Thrilling Tragedy:
The Royal Nonesuch
Admission 50 cents
LADIES AND CHILDREN NOT ADMITTED!!!

"There," the duke said with great pride. "If that last line doesn't pack the house, I don't know Arkansas!"

The duke was right. That night the courthouse was jammed so tight there wasn't room for a chihuahua to squeeze in.

First the duke made a little speech about how this was the most thrillingest tragedy of all time. Then the curtain flew up and *The Royal Nonesuch* began. Now, I wasn't very experienced at seeing plays, but that show had to be the worst show that any man or animal had ever witnessed.

The king stood on stage, nearly naked. His elderly body was painted with rings and stripes, colored every shade of the rainbow. Then the king pranced about on all fours, like some kind of crazy horse. He bucked and kicked and shook his head. After about five wild minutes of this, the curtain came down.

That was the whole show!

There was so much booing you wouldn't have heard a pack of St. Bernards bark. Angry folks were shouting out things like:

"Is that all?"

"We want our money back!"

"We ought to cover those two actors with tar and feathers!"

Through the performance, my nose had picked up some interesting odors. I realized why. As the duke and king proudly took their bows, men heaved eggs and rotten vegetables and even a few dead rats at the stage.

All of a sudden, people rushed the stage, yelling about getting revenge for being gypped. The duke and king tore out the back way, and I tore out the front. The three of us ran fast as lightning for the raft. Soon as we jumped on board, Jim pushed off and we went riding down the river.

As Jim and I steered the raft, the duke and king fell down, laughing about the money they had made in Brickville. I laughed too, but I was also ashamed for helping out with the silly show.

"Huck," Jim whispered as he dipped his pole in the water, "do you reckon we'll be meeting any more royalty on this trip?"

"Oh, I doubt it," I replied.

"I hope not," Jim mumbled. "Royal folks are an awful lot of trouble."

I pulled off my hat and let Jim rub the top of my head—for good luck.

And our raft kept drifting onward.

Looks like Jim and Huck have hooked up with a couple of crooks. Good thing there aren't any crooks in Oakdale. Or are there?

Chapter Seven

Wishbone and David cut across the lawn of Oakdale Elementary School. A PTA carnival was in full swing. Small groups of kids and parents swarmed around the brightly decorated booths. Parents working the event were decked out in funny costumes. Wishbone's ears perked up at music floating through the air. Then came the tempting odors. His nose tingled at the smells of popcorn, cotton candy, and, best of all, hot dogs.

"Where is she?" David asked. "I've got to find her."

"Say, how about we get a couple of hot dogs?" Wishbone suggested.

"Emily goes in my room all the time," David said, thinking aloud. "I'll bet she borrowed Gilbert's Zip-T. She must have. Emily? Emily!"

"Hot dogs? Hot dogs!" Wishbone echoed.

Hearing a loud growl, Wishbone spun around. He found himself staring up at a purple-faced lion who stood on two legs. The terrier reared back, ready to bolt. Then he realized it wasn't really a lion. It was David's little sister, Emily. She had paid a visit to the face-painting booth.

"There you are." David turned to his sister. "Where's Mom?"

"Over there." She pointed to the balloon booth. "What are you and Wishbone doing here?"

"Looking for you," David said. "We need to talk."

Emily turned away as a loud bell went off in one of the booths. "That's the game with the milk bottles. Who won a prize?"

"Emily, listen. Did you take something out of my room this morning? After I got home from Lisa's house? Maybe while I ran out to get my tool box in the garage?"

Emily waved at a friend.

"Emily, this is very important," David said firmly. "Did you take something from my room?"

"Nooo," Emily said, looking sheepishly at her shoes.

Wishbone caught the scent of nervousness coming from Emily.

"I think she's lying," Wishbone whispered to David. "She must be the Zip-T thief."

David gave her a stern look. "Are you sure?"

"Oh, look!" Emily said with a gap-toothed smile. "They just blew up a bunch of new balloons. I want that foil one."

She's changing the subject, Wishbone thought. *A sure sign of guilt. These five-year-olds can be very sneaky.*

David knelt down to Emily's level. "Listen, if you

did take something from my room, I need to know about it. I promise I won't be mad at you."

"Can I just go and get a balloon?" Emily asked.

"Emily, please," David said, growing impatient.

Emily's purple face puckered in a frown. "All right, but don't get mad. Because I did take something from your room."

Ah-ha, Wishbone thought. *The missing computer!*

"Oh, great," David said, closing his eyes with relief.

"You're happy?" Emily looked puzzled. "Maybe I should take your candy bars more often."

"Candy bars?" David asked.

Emily scratched at the purple whiskers on one cheek. "I was passing your room and I saw a candy bar on your desk. So I borrowed it. Well . . . I ate it."

"Is that all?" David demanded. "Didn't you also take a small computer device? A purple thing with a small screen on it?"

"No," Emily insisted. "Just the candy bar."

David nodded with disappointment. "Okay, I believe you. Thanks for being honest."

"Mom! Tina is getting *two* balloons!" Emily cried, skipping away toward the balloon booth.

"Tough break," Wishbone told David. "That means the Zip-T is still missing. Hey, to cheer ourselves up, how about—"

David headed to the refreshment stand. Wishbone followed, the smells of grilling hot dogs sending a hunger signal to his stomach. Wishbone feared that David would be getting nothing more exciting than some lemonade. But luckily, David bought two tasty-smelling hot dogs.

Wishbone looked up expectantly. *Ah, David, I do believe you were reading my mind.*

David kept one hot dog for himself and set the other on the ground. Wishbone ate his hot dog so fast he thought he might have set a new record, even for himself.

"David, that was mighty nice of you," Wishbone said with a burp. "And if you buy me another hot dog, it would be even nicer."

David was too busy eating his hot dog to hear the request.

As David and Wishbone headed away from the carnival, the music and laughter faded. Soon they came to the green lawns and trees of Jackson Park. A summery hush hung over the area.

David sat on a rock, and Wishbone sat beside him.

"Emily was my last hope," David muttered to himself. "If she didn't take the Zip-T, nobody did. It's just lost. And I can't even buy Gilbert a new one. Even if I

saved every cent of my allowance, it would take years."

David rested his head in his hands, looking upset.

"Ah, cheer up," Wishbone said, trying to be supportive. "Listen, when you're grounded, I'll visit you every day. I'll even sneak some food in for you. Burgers, candy bars, kibble, you name it. And if you need help digging an escape tunnel through your floor, I'm the best digger in the business."

David reached down to scratch Wishbone's neck. "Mmm . . . a little to the left," Wishbone said.

"Right now," David told Wishbone, "I feel like you're my only friend in the world."

"Same here, pal," Wishbone replied. "You would never let anyone dress me up in dog clothes."

Wishbone suddenly saw something glinting beyond a patch of trees. A blue car had pulled into a lane at the western edge of the park.

That's odd, Wishbone thought. *Even though this is a park, people never* park *here.* He watched as two people climbed out of the car. Then a little pink creature appeared.

Curious, Wishbone walked toward the car. *Oh no!* he thought with alarm. *It's those people with the dog clothes! And they brought that poodle in the pink tutu! Why are they here? Are they coming after me?*

I can't seem to get away from Queenie the poodle, and Huck can't seem to get away from the duke and the king.

Chapter Eight

As another morning dawned, we tied the raft near another one-horse town. The duke and king put their heads together, trying to come up with a new money-making scheme. They figured their show, *The Royal Nonesuch,* was too risky for the time because word might spread about what a gyp it was.

To make ourselves look more respectable, the duke bought store clothes for himself, me, and the king. He also came up with a way for us to travel during the day. He dressed Jim in one of his Shakespearean costumes—an old-style gown, a white wig, and a white beard. Then he painted Jim's face and hands bright blue and hung a sign near Jim that announced: "Sick Arab—but he's harmless, most of the time."

Jim didn't look like a runaway slave anymore. In fact, he looked scary enough to make my whiskers twitch.

"That will keep anyone from thinking he's a runaway slave," the duke said, admiring his artistic work.

Then the duke, king, and I wandered through the town. Soon we came across an innocent-looking young fellow who was on his way to the steamboat landing.

"Are you the Wilks brothers?" the fellow said, pointing at the king and then the duke.

"No, I am the Reverend Alexander Blodgett," the king said in a phony voice. "And these are my . . . assistants. But who is this Mr. Wilks?"

"Well, a gentleman in town named Peter Wilks passed away last night," the fellow explained, setting down a suitcase. "His two brothers, Harvey and William, were coming all the way from England to be with their brother in his final days. But now they'll be lucky if they make it in time for the funeral. Harvey's a minister, and William is a mute. That's what I hear. But those two brothers have lived in England so long, no one in these parts knows what they really look like."

"Tell me this," the king said, lowering his voice. "Did this dead man, Peter Wilks, leave behind a will?"

"Yes, he did," the young man answered. "He left his house and slaves and some money to his three daughters. But he left all the rest of his money to Harvey and William. I hear it amounts to several thousand dollars. Too bad I won't be able to make the funeral, but I'm leaving for South America today."

"Hmm . . . very interesting," the king said, stroking his beard.

The duke stroked his mustache, also looking interested.

Nervously, I scratched my side. I knew what those two rascals were thinking. The king kept talking to the man, trying to get other information about Peter Wilks and his brothers.

As soon as the young man left, the duke and king hatched their plan. They would pretend to be the two Wilks brothers so they could collect the dead man's money. Since Harvey Wilks was from England, the king practiced his English accent. Since William Wilks was a mute, the duke practiced not saying anything.

They told me to pretend to be Harvey's servan-boy, Adolphus. I didn't want to go along with the scheme, but I was afraid that the duke and king might make some serious trouble for Jim if I didn't. So I went along. Jim stayed with the raft.

Two hours later, we showed up at the handsome house that had belonged to Peter Wilks. A lot of folks were gathered in the parlor, mourning the dead man. The king introduced himself and the duke as Harvey and William Wilks, and they were given a warm wel-come. Then the king and duke went to the coffin, which lay in the middle of the room, supported by two chairs.

"Alas, alas, alas!" the king moaned in a phony English accent. "Our poor brother is gone, gone, gone!"

Since the duke was pretending to be a mute, he just gurgled out babyish things like, "Goo goo goo!"

Then the king and duke both bust out blubbering so loud they could probably be heard down in New Or-leans. The women dabbed their eyes with handker-chiefs and the men nodded solemnly. Everyone bought the act. Myself, I just lay on the floor.

Peter Wilks had three daughters, Joanna, Susan, and Mary Jane. At nineteen, Mary Jane was the eldest, not to mention the prettiest. I confess, the very sight of her made my tail skip about with excitement. Her skin was smooth as silk and her red hair glowed like a sunset. After a while, Mary Jane handed the king a bag filled with something jingly.

"This is most of my father's money," Mary Jane said, blinking back tears. "Nearly six thousand dollars in gold coins. Father meant for this to go to you and William. And naturally, you two are welcome to stay in this house as long as you like."

The king and duke eyed that bag of gold the way a dog gazes at a pork chop on a plate.

"Bless you, child," the king said taking the bag in his greedy hand. "My brother and I will see that you and your sisters are never alone in this cold world."

What a lie that was. I knew the king and duke would steal away with the money first chance they got. It made me ashamed of the human race. Right there and then, I decided I would steal the money from the king and duke then give it back to the three sisters. I just needed to do it in such a way that the duke and king would never *know* that I had done it.

Soon after dinner, the king and duke headed to the town's tavern with some of the local menfolk. I crept upstairs to the king's bedroom. After some sniffing around, I found the bag of gold stashed away in the closet.

I grabbed the money bag with my teeth and pulled. It didn't budge because it was so heavy. I tried again without much luck. Then I pretended that the bag was stuffed with a bunch of bones just waiting for me to bury them. I gave another tug and sure enough, that bag came with me.

I dragged the bag out of the room and down the stairs, trying not to let the coins clang. Soon I was creeping through the parlor, heading for the front door, when . . . I heard footsteps. There wasn't no time to get outside. I needed to hide that money or someone might think *I* was the one stealing it.

I glanced around for a hiding place. My eyes stopped on the coffin. The lid of the coffin had been left open so people could say proper goodbyes to the dead man inside. Using all my might, I heaved the bag in the air, aiming for the coffin. With a thud, the bag landed smack on the dead man, probably right across his chest. Then, luckily, the lid of the coffin fell shut.

That very second, Mary Jane Wilkes entered the parlor, wearing a nightgown.

"Adolphus," Mary Jane cried with surprise, "what are you doing here?"

"Uh, well, I was just . . . paying my respects."

Immediately, I realized that I had forgotten to speak with an English accent. Mary Jane realized it too.

"Adolphus," Mary Jane said, her brows creasing. "I thought you were from England. But you sure don't sound like it anymore."

"No, no, Miss Mary Jane, I'm really from England."

"Then why aren't you speaking with an accent?"

"Uh, well, that's a very good question. And . . . I'll tell you the answer."

"Yes?"

I gave my side a scratch, stalling for time. Finally an answer came to me.

"People in England don't naturally speak with an English accent," I explained. "They just pretend they have an accent to make themselves sound fancier."

"Adolphus," Mary Jane said, staring down at me with her lovely eyes, "I don't think you're being honest with me."

By the light of the room's flickering candles, she looked more red-haired and beautiful than ever. She also looked too intelligent to be fooled. So I fessed up the full truth, telling Mary Jane how the duke and the king were only pretending to be her uncles so they could get their hands on her father's money.

"Those dirty scalawags," Mary Jane exclaimed, flushing with anger. "They ought to be—"

"Shhh," I whispered. "I don't want them knowing that I squealed on them. Then they might cause trouble for me and this runaway . . . uh, this other fellow I'm friendly with."

Mary Jane knelt down to me. "Well, I don't want to cause trouble for you and your friend. What should I do?"

I walked in a circle for a few moments, thinking real hard. Finally I figured out a plan.

"Listen," I said, "first thing after the funeral tomorrow morning, I want you to leave town for the day. Can you do that?"

"Yes, I'll go stay with the Lothrop family. But why is that necessary?"

"Because you're too innocent to lie, Miss Mary

Jane. The duke and king will see in your face that you know the truth about them. And they'll figure out I was the one who told you. So you need to stay gone until around eleven at night. That'll be the best time for me and my friend to slip away from this area."

"I'll do exactly as you say. But what should I do when I return around eleven?"

"Tell the townsfolk just what I told you. They'll see that the duke and king get thrown in jail. When it comes time for their trial, send word to the town of Brickville. Folks up there can tell all about how the king and duke fooled them with a show called *The Royal Nonesuch.*"

Mary Jane covered her face with her hands. "Oh, dear me, I feel so stupid for giving those two brutes my father's money. They've probably already hidden it somewhere!"

"As a matter of fact," I said proudly, "I stole the money away from them."

"Where did you put it?" she asked, uncovering her face.

"I tossed it in . . . " I stopped myself. Suddenly I felt real silly about where the money was hidden. I didn't think the dead man would mind having the money on his chest, but I was afraid Mary Jane might not like it too much. Even so, Mary Jane had to know where the money was located. So I jumped up onto a little desk and wrote a note, explaining exactly where the money bag was hidden. I folded the note in half and took it in my mouth.

"Does this tell where the money is hidden?" Mary Jane asked, taking the note from my mouth.

"Yes, but please don't read it until you get back to-morrow night. Some of the townsfolk will help you fetch the money."

"Adolphus, how can I ever thank you?" Mary Jane said, her voice sweet as strawberry pie.

I nearly melted like butter, smiling up at her.

"Thank you, dear Adolphus." She rested her silky cheek against my fur. "You have done a truly noble deed tonight. I will not forget you. I promise to pray for you every day of my life."

My heart felt like it was already soaring halfway to heaven.

The funeral took place the following morning. The coffin was buried, miraculously without anyone seeing the bag of gold inside. As planned, Mary Jane left immediately after the burial, without saying a word to anyone. I explained to her sisters that she had to visit a friend who had come down with a really bad case of the mumps. A bunch of townsfolk hung around the house all day, telling stories about what a swell fellow Peter Wilks had been. Every so often, the king would break out weeping, and the duke would gurgle out a few more "goo goos."

Most of the day, I lay on a rug pretending to sleep. I was planning to high-tail it for the raft as soon as the clock in the corner struck eleven that night. But as often happens, something interfered with my plans.

Just as darkness fell, two finely dressed gentlemen showed up at the house. One was about the king's age, the other was about the duke's age.

In a perfect English accent, the older man announced, "Greetings, everyone. I am Harvey Wilks and this is my brother, William Wilks. We are late due to an unfortunate accident on our steamboat. Can anyone tell us if our brother, Peter, is still alive?"

The king and duke exchanged a worried look.

In his phony English accent, the king announced, "Peter Wilks was just buried this morning. But you and this other gentleman cannot be Peter's brothers because myself and this gentlemen beside me are his brothers!"

"Goo goo goo!" the duke added.

The real William Wilks frowned at the duke.

"These men are frauds and liars!" the real Harvey Wilks said, pointing at the duke and king.

"No, *these* men are frauds and liars!" the king said, pointing at the real brothers.

The place went crazy with confusion. The folks in

HUCKLEBERRY DOG

the parlor knew that one pair of brothers had to be a
fake. They just didn't know which one. The real Harvey Wilks claimed that his dead brother had his initials
tattooed on his chest. The undertaker happened to be
present, but he couldn't remember seeing anything
tattooed on Peter's chest. At that, the king claimed that
Peter didn't have his initials tattooed on his chest because he had a blue arrow tattooed there.

It was decided that there was only one way to un-
tangle the situation. The dead man would have to be
dug out of the ground.

Off we all went to the graveyard. Men grabbed a
hold of each of the four brothers. The menfolk didn't
want the imposters, whoever they turned out to be,
slipping away from the scene of their crime. My tail
swished about with deep concern. I knew that the coffin would reveal something more startling than a *tat-
too* on the dead man's chest!

By the time we reached the graveyard, cold rain
soaked my fur. Several men went to work at the grave
site with shovels. After an agonizing wait, the coffin
was pulled up from its resting place. The lid was forced
open and . . .

Lightning flashed, throwing a white glare across
the scene.

"Hang it all!" someone sang out, "There's a bag of
gold on Peter's chest!"

Thunderstruck with amazement, everyone closed
in on the coffin for closer look. This was my chance. I
leaped out of the arms of the man holding me and flew
away from the graveyard. Rain slashed and the wind
thrashed, but I kept my four paws pounding the

ground like a champion racehorse.

Just as I was running past the Wilks house, a light appeared in Mary Jane's window. I realized Mary Jane had returned home. I skidded to a stop. Gazing at her window, I watched the candle-flame dance merrily behind the lace curtain. More than anything, I wanted to go visit Mary Jane and let her scratch me behind the ears some more. She was the best girl I had ever met. My ears drooped, knowing I would never see her again.

Off I ran, not stopping until I found the raft and jumped aboard. Lightning streaked the sky. A man with a long white beard and a horrible blue face towered over me. I was so terrified, I stumbled backward and tumbled overboard. Then a pair of hands fished me out of the water. As I tried to wriggle away, I realized the blue man was only Jim, disguised as a sick Arab.

"I guess I fooled you," Jim said, having himself a good guffaw.

"Laugh about it later!" I shouted. "Right now, we need to shove off! No time to lose!"

Less than two seconds later, the raft was sliding silently down the river. My tail wagged with relief as I pulled the pole through the rain-spattered water. At long last, Jim and I had escaped from the king and the duke.

But . . . my ears lifted, hearing the sound of paddles. I whipped around to see a canoe following us. A burst of lightning showed me who was in the canoe—the duke and the king!

"Wait for us!" the duke hollered.

"We're a-coming!" the king bellowed.

I lay down and covered my eyes with my front paw. It didn't seem we would *ever* stop being hounded by those two crooks.

Chapter Nine

The king and duke were so afraid of being caught, they made us travel day and night, not stopping anywhere. The river took us way down South, a mighty long way from home.

The summer weather grew so hot, my tongue was always panting halfway out of my mouth. Along the shore, the trees began to be dripping with something called Spanish moss. It made the woods look like spooky green ghosts who wore shaggy beards.

One moonless night, while the duke and king slept in the wigwam, I lay resting on the raft. As I listened to the whispering of the wind, I heard another sound mixing in with it. My ears led me to the back of the raft. Jim sat there, moaning to himself with his head between his knees.

"What's the matter?" I asked, nudging him gently.

"Oh, Huck, I miss my family," Jim said, wiping a tear from his cheek. "My wife and little Johnny and little Lizabeth. Bless her heart—Lizabeth, she's deaf. She can't hear a single word. That means she really needs her daddy there looking after her."

"I guess she does," I said softly.

Jim held a fist to his forehead, obviously in great pain. "Whenever I think about my children, it feels like my heart might break all to pieces. I've got to find a way to see them again!"

I took off my hat to let Jim rub the top of my head. Both of us had come to hope that like rubbing a genie's lamp, it would bring us good luck.

More days dragged by. Finally the duke and king figured they had put enough distance between themselves and the scenes of their last few crimes. They tried all kinds of money-making schemes—doctoring, dentistry, dancing lessons, speech lessons, fortune telling, and, now and then, they'd put on a few performances of *The Royal Nonesuch*. But they weren't having much success. Soon the two scoundrels were flat broke.

They lay around the raft a lot, trying to come up with some new kind of scheme. When they took to whispering real low, Jim and I grew suspicious.

"I'll bet those two are up to something really bad this time," Jim told me. "Like robbing a store or making fake money or . . . something."

"Whatever it is," I said, "let's not have anything to do with it. First chance we get, let's shake these fellows loose."

I gave my tail a shake to emphasize my point.

Just before dawn one morning, we hid the raft

near a one-horse town called Pikesville. The king went ashore to have a peek at the townsfolk. But when noon rolled around, the king still wasn't back. The duke grabbed me by the scruff of my neck, saying we should go look for the king. I didn't argue, figuring this might give Jim and me a chance to slip away on our own.

After tramping through the dusty town, the duke and I found the king in a tavern. My nose twitched at the smell of sweat and cheap liquor. The king was so drunk he could barely stand up.

"How'd it go?" the duke asked.

"Good," the king mumbled.

I tilted my head, not sure what they were discussing.

The duke put out his hand. "Where's my share of the money?"

"Gone."

"Gone?"

The king drained a glass of whiskey. "I drank some of it away and I gambled the rest away."

The duke shook the king roughly by the shoulders. "You crazy fool! Now we're broke again! That means we have to risk putting on *The Royal Nonesuch* tonight!"

"Don't look at me!" the king said, raising a fist to the duke. "After all, you're the one who put all that gold in the coffin so you could fetch it later all to yourself!"

"I've told you a hundred times," the duke yelled, shoving the king across the room, "I didn't put that gold in the coffin! But the more you bring it up, the more I think *you* were the one who put it there!"

The duke and king fell to cussing back and forth so much they didn't see me anymore. I sneaked out, quiet as a mouse. Then I moved my four legs for all they were worth.

When I reached the raft, I hollered, "Set her loose, Jim! Finally we're free of those two crooks! Jim! Jim, where are you?"

But Jim wasn't on the raft and he wasn't inside the wigwam either. I yelled and barked and howled to the blue sky. But there was no sign of Jim anywhere.

Jim was gone!

I knew Jim would never leave the raft unless something really terrible had happened. Sagging down onto the raft, I whimpered. In all my days, I'd never felt quite so lonesome.

Soon I wandered into the woods, hoping to find some answers about where Jim could be. I ran across a boy just a bit younger than myself.

"Pardon me," I said politely. "Did you happen to see a big black man who goes by the name of Jim?"

"Yes," the boy said. "He's a runaway slave."

"What makes you think so?"

"Everyone in town knows," the boy said, talking as slow as molasses. "About an hour ago, a bald old fellow with a beard came by. He said he had captured a slave who had run away from the St. Jacques plantation in New Orleans. He showed a poster that said there was a three-hundred-dollar reward for the slave."

"And then what?" I said, my tail swishing with impatience.

"This old fellow said he didn't have time to wait around for the slave's owner to come and hand over the reward. So he offered to turn the slave over to anyone willing to pay forty dollars."

"Did anyone take the offer?"

"Yep," the boy replied, "Silas Phelps and some other men went down to the old fellow's raft. The slave was there and he fit the description on that poster. Mr. Phelps paid the old fellow forty dollars and took the slave. He's got the slave locked away at his plantation. It's about two miles below town."

"What will they do with the slave?" I asked.

The boy shrugged. "I guess they'll keep him prisoner until the rightful owner can come from New Orleans to claim him."

I thanked the boy, then trudged back to the raft, feeling as if each of my paws weighed a hundred pounds. Jim was doomed.

Everything made sense now. The old fellow was the king. He must have had the "Wanted" poster printed up somewhere without me seeing it. The king had sold Jim that morning, then given him away while the duke made me help him look for the king. The forty dollars the king received for Jim must have been the money the king and duke were arguing about at the tavern.

With every step, I grew madder and madder until I was burning hot. After all this long journey to get Jim free, everything was ruined. Why? Because that greedy king and duke had sold Jim out for a dirty forty dollars!

The raft was still empty when I got to it. I lay down and rested my muzzle on my front paws. I had some serious thinking to do.

Let's see . . . the way things are now, there's no telling where Jim may end up. But if Jim has to be a slave, maybe it's better for him to be Miss Watson's slave. That way he won't be too far away from his wife and children. Maybe I should write Miss Watson, explaining where Jim is located.

Then I thought otherwise.

No, wait. Miss Watson was planning to sell Jim to a slave-trader down in New Orleans. Then the trader in New Orleans will sell Jim to the highest bidder and he might end up . . . anywhere.

Suddenly, I felt as if the heavens were staring down at me, and all those angels with all their harps were frowning on Huck Finn. They were frowning because I was more concerned with a slave's feelings than I was with the law of the country.

I decided, right then and there, I would do my best to lead a more decent life. So I put my two front paws together and tried to pray. I was planning to pray for the strength to turn Jim in to his rightful owner. But the words wouldn't come. I guess that's because my heart didn't really want to betray Jim. You can't pray a lie.

Then I got a bright idea. I would write the letter to Miss Watson telling her about Jim—and *then* see if I could pray. Right away, I felt light as a feather, like my troubles were almost gone.

I got a piece of paper, took a pen and wrote:

Miss Watson,

Your runaway slave, Jim, is down here in Arkansas. Two miles below the town of Pikesville. Mr. Phelps has him and I'm sure he will turn him over for some reward money.

Huck Finn

Soon as I finished writing, I lay down again in my thinking position. For the first time ever, I felt all washed clean of sin. It was a nice feeling, like I'd just rid my fur from an attack of fleas.

Now when I die, I thought peacefully, *I'll go to heaven instead of that really hot place that rhymes with "bell."*

And then my thoughts floated in another direction—to all the time I spent going down the river with Jim.

We went through moonlight and storms. We talked and laughed and sang songs. I've got nothing but warm feelings about Jim. Remember how glad he was to see me after we thought each other had been killed by the steamboat? Remember how he was so good at petting and scratching and rubbing me? Remember how he said I was the best friend he ever had?

Then my eyes fell on the letter.

Suddenly I seemed to hear my conscience whispering inside my ear. *Go on, send the letter. Send it, send it, send it. You know it's the respectable thing to do, Huckleberry. You know it's the only way to keep yourself out of that really hot place that rhymes with "bell."*

I stared straight at that letter.

I knew I had to decide, forever, between two very important things. On the one paw, there was the right thing—what my conscience wanted me to do. On the other paw, there was the wrong thing—what my heart wanted me to do. My tail was flicking back and forth with a dreadful fear.

"All right, then," I shouted out loud. "I'll *go* to hell!"

My heart had won the battle.

I grabbed that letter between my paws and ripped it to shreds with my sharp teeth. It was an awful, wicked, sinful thing I was doing, but I didn't care. Jim was my friend, and I wasn't going to lift a paw to send him back into slavery. Matter of fact, I was going to do everything in my power to help that man get free!

I moved the raft to a spot where the duke and king wouldn't find it. As night fell, I lay down and passed some time chewing on a piece of driftwood I'd fished out of the river.

A little later, I heard an awful racket—whooping, yelling, and the clanging of tin pots. Through the trees, I saw a group of people hurrying along, some carrying blazing torches. At the front of the group were two figures that looked like a pair of overgrown chickens. I realized two unfortunate people had been covered with sticky black tar and feathers. Tar and feathering, that was something folks in those parts did to other folks when they felt they had been cheated in a big-time way.

My tail jumped when I realized who the two overgrown chickens were—the duke and the king. Finally, they had been caught. I guess they had put on their *Royal Nonesuch* show and couldn't get away from the angry customers afterward. I felt bad for the two scoundrels, even though they had done Jim wrong. One thing I was learning on this trip—human beings could be awful cruel to each other.

When the racket faded away, I curled up and

went to sleep. With the rise of morning, I would see about setting Jim free.

And back in Oakdale, I've caught sight of the Peabodys and their poodle in a pink tutu!

Chapter Ten

"David!" Wishbone called as he rushed back toward his friend. "We have to beat it out of here! You know the people I'm trying to escape? They're right behind those trees!"

"What are you afraid of?" David knelt beside the dog.

"Them!" Wishbone said, pointing his muzzle toward the Peabodys. "They're dying to dress me up!"

David looked toward the western edge of the park. Mr. and Mrs. Peabody huddled beside their blue car. For some reason, they were both peering into Mrs. Peabody's large purse. Queenie scampered around their feet, as if expecting a treat. Wishbone noticed an empty green car parked right behind the blue car.

"That lane is an odd place to park a car," David said, mostly talking to himself. "It's almost like those people don't want their car to be seen."

David hid behind a tree to get a closer look at the Peabodys. Slowly, Wishbone followed.

"I've seen those two before," David said softly. "Oh, yeah, I remember. When I got home from Lisa's this morning, they were there. Mom said they were going door to door, selling stuff for dogs. The lady was coming out of our bathroom when I got home."

"That must have been right before they came to our house," Wishbone told David. "But Mrs. Peabody asked to use our restroom too."

The man reached into his wife's purse and pulled out a purple object.

"Hey," David gasped. "That looks like a Zip-T. And it's a purple one, just like Gilbert's. Whoa."

Wishbone gave a tug at David's sock, then said, "David, let's get out of here before they see us."

Mr. Peabody returned the computer to her purse, then pulled out something else—a portable radio.

"She has all kinds of electronic gizmos in that purse," David said, squinting. "What's going on here?"

"Don't get too close!" Wishbone urged. "My dignity is at stake!"

"Hey," David said, staring at the Peabodys. "That *is* Gilbert's Zip-T. I bet those two are thieves!"

"What?" Wishbone said, perking up his ears.

"Sure, that's it!" David said with growing excitement. "They go around pretending to sell dog clothes. The lady goes off toward the bathroom, but she's really stealing stuff. She must have sneaked into my room and put the Zip-T into her purse."

Wishbone pawed at David's leg. "By golly, I think you're right. That's why the lady asked to use our bathroom too. And I'll bet that poodle is the mastermind of the scam!"

Mr. Peabody opened the trunk of the green car and set the purse inside.

"That's why they have two cars," David continued. "They put all the stolen goods in the green car because everyone in town saw only the blue car. And now's the time for their getaway. I have to stop them. Maybe I can delay them until someone shows up to help. Come on, Wishbone."

Wishbone followed David as he moved through the trees, calling, "Hey, hello!"

Mr. Peabody slammed the trunk of the green car just as they reached the lane.

"Uh...hello," Mrs. Peabody replied in a nervous voice.

Mr. Peabody looked over curiously.

Queenie glared at Wishbone, mistrust in her beady eyes.

"Are you the people going around selling clothes for dogs?" David asked. "A friend told me about you."

"Yes, we are," Mrs. Peabody said. "I believe we've already met this dog. Isn't this little Wishbone?"

"Little?" Wishbone said, pointing his head toward Queenie. "Who are you calling *little*, lady?"

"No," David said quickly, "Wishbone is another dog in town who looks a lot like this one. This is *my* dog . . . Ralph."

Wishbone turned to David. "Who are you calling *Ralph?*"

"My name is . . . . Norton," David told the Peabodys.

Oh, I see, Wishbone thought. *We're using fake names now. Very clever, David. You don't want the Peabodys to know that they've already visited both of our houses.*

"We're Mr. and Mrs. Peabody," Mrs. Peabody said cheerfully. "And this is our darling Queenie."

David knelt down to pat the poodle in the pink tutu. "That's some outfit. You know, Ralph could use some new clothes. Mind if I take a look?"

Mr. Peabody's smile faded. "We're kind of in a hurry."

"It'll only take a minute," David insisted. "I don't take long to make up my mind."

Ah, I get it. David isn't really going to buy anything. He's just trying to stop them from getting away with the stolen goods.

The Peabodys exchanged a look. Wishbone could imagine what they were thinking. They didn't want to hang around any longer than necessary, but refusing to show the clothes might look suspicious. Mr. Peabody reached into the blue car and pulled out the big suitcase.

"Always have time for a sale," he said, setting it on the ground and opening it.

David pulled out a dark blue outfit. It had gold

buttons shaped like anchors and a square flap of a collar.

"That's the Sailor Sam uniform," Mrs. Peabody said, talking quickly now. "Perfect for Ralph. Do you want it?"

David frowned. "Do you mind if Ralph tries it on?"

"Forget it," Wishbone whispered to David. "It's bad enough I have to pretend my name is Ralph. But I put my paw down at putting this thing on. No self-respecting dog wears—"

"Sure, go ahead," Mr. Peabody said. "Just make it quick."

David turned to Wishbone. "Okay, pal. Lift your front paws."

"Norton, I'm begging you," Wishbone whispered. "I don't want to wear this outfit. I know I'm undercover and I'm playing a role. But what if my pals see me? I'll be laughed out of town. Try to see my side of this situation."

Queenie inched closer to Wishbone. Her tail wagged happily, and her tiny teeth formed a grin. She seemed to be saying, "Welcome to the couture club, buster!"

Wishbone looked up at David, who held the outfit out to him.

David is one of my best friends. He's always there for me when I need him, willing to scratch my back or feed me a treat. Heck, he even bought me a hot dog today. If I put this goofy outfit on, it might delay the Peabodys long enough for David to get help. And that means David might get back the Zip-T back. Which would save him from big trouble. All right, I'll do it!

   Wishbone lifted his front paws, allowing David to slip the sailor outfit over his head.

   This is soooo embarrassing! But what can I say? I guess I'll do anything to get David out of trouble. Huck's the same way. He's about to risk all four paws to help Jim become a free man.

Chapter Eleven

The next morning, I walked to the Phelps plantation, where Jim was being held prisoner. It was hot and sunshiny and quiet as a Sunday. Bugs and flies buzzed through the air. I had to keep swatting them away with my paws and tail. I didn't know what I was going to do exactly. I just trusted that the right idea would pop in my head at the proper time. It usually did.

The Phelps place was a small cotton plantation. A fence surrounded a yard that had a log house for the family and a few smaller cabins for the slaves. Outside the fence there was a garden and a watermelon patch and the cotton fields.

As soon as I passed through the fence, a lady with her hair in a bun came rushing out of the house. I figured it was Mrs. Phelps. She was followed by a few little children.

"It's you at last!" the lady called out to me. "Oh, your Aunt Sally is so glad to see you!"

I had no idea what she was talking about, so I just kind of nodded.

The lady took off my hat. "You don't look as much like your mother as I expected. But for gracious sakes, I'm so pleased to see you. It's been years since I've had a look at you, dear boy. I could just eat you up. Children, say howdy to your cousin Tom."

Pretty soon an old farmer came ambling through the yard. I figured this was the lady's husband, Mr. Phelps. He would be the one who had paid the forty dollars to keep Jim until Jim's rightful owner showed up with the reward money.

"Who's this?" the farmer asked.

"Why, it's our nephew, Tom Sawyer!" the lady exclaimed. "He's changed since we last saw him. His steamboat must have just come in. Tom, you remember your Uncle Silas, don't you?"

By jings, I could have jumped out of my fur. I realized that these folks were relatives of Tom Sawyer, and Tom was expected to come visiting there that very day! How do you like that for luck?

The man knelt down and gave my paw a shake. I figured I could pretend to be Tom Sawyer for a little while. I wasn't sure what would happen when Tom actually showed up. Uncle Silas said he would go down to the ferry landing with me to help with my bags. But I told him I could handle things just fine on my own.

So I borrowed a horse-drawn wagon and rode it toward the steamboat landing in town. Halfway there, another wagon approached and I saw my old friend Tom Sawyer sitting on it, right beside a driver. The second he saw me, Tom's face went white with terror.

"Huck, I've never done you any harm," Tom cried out hoarsely. "Why are you back to haunt me with your ghost?"

I took Tom aside so the driver couldn't hear me. Then I explained how I had faked my death to escape from my Pap. Tom, of course, loved my story because it was all filled with mystery, like something out of one of his books. Then I told Tom about Jim and how I needed to break him loose from the Phelps plantation.

"But Jim is a—" Tom began.

"I know what you're about to say," I told Tom. "That helping a slave escape is a dirty business. But I've decided to do it, all the same. If you don't want to help me, I'll understand."

Tom's eyes lit up with glee. "Of course, I'll help you, Huck. Escapes are one of my specialties!"

To be honest, I was a little disappointed in Tom. I never figured him to be a low-down breaker of the law . . . like me.

Anyway, Tom and I worked out a plan. Since I, Huck, was supposed to be Tom, Tom would pretend to be Tom's little brother, Sid. Then we moved Tom's bags from his wagon to mine and we both rode back to the Phelps plantation.

"Oh, gracious," Aunt Sally said when I explained that Tom was really my little brother, Sid. "My sister, Polly, didn't mention anything in her letters about Sid coming along."

Tom jumped right in with an answer. "Well, it wasn't intended for me to come. But I begged my Aunt Polly, and finally she gave in. Tom came up to the house first so I could surprise you. We wanted to pull

105

off a first-rate surprise."

"I see," Aunt Sally said, looking us both over. "Well, Tom and Sid, I welcome both of you to our humble home."

Soon Tom and I went to our bedroom but we didn't go to sleep. Instead we climbed out the window and slid down a lightning rod that ran up the side of the house. Creeping through the night, we went to a small log hut that sat by the back fence. Tom had a suspicion that Jim was locked away in that hut. Sure enough, the door was padlocked.

I crouched down low and stole a peek through the crack under the door. The place was pitch-dark, and I heard snoring inside. My nose can identify folks pretty well just by their scent. And my nose told me that Jim was the one doing the snoring.

"Jim," I whispered. "It's me, Huck."

After a moment, I heard Jim whisper back. "Huck, oh, it's so good to hear your voice. Where did you—"

"Shhh," I whispered. "I can't explain everything right now. But Tom Sawyer is here with me. Don't you worry about a thing, Jim. Tom and I are going to set you free. Only don't let on to anyone that you know us. I better go now."

Tom and I went inside a small storage shack that butted up against Jim's hut. We figured this would be a safe place for us to talk.

"We need a plan," Tom said eagerly.

Both of us thought a few moments.

Finally I said, "How about we steal the key that unlocks the padlock? Then we can just let Jim out."

"Well, sure, that might work," Tom said. "But it's

too darn simple. There's no style to it. We need some kind of fancy plan that would make even Robin Hood proud of us. By jings, I know. We can dig a tunnel from this here shack into Jim's hut."

I gave my front paws a proud look. "Sure, that's how I escaped from the shack where my Pap kept me. When it comes to digging, I'm about as good as they come."

"It can't be easy, though. We'll use rusty pocket knives."

"Why can't I dig the way I know best?"

Tom let out a frustrated sigh. "Because we've got to do everything the way they do it in the adventure books. Otherwise it's too simple. There's a book about a fellow named the Count of Monte Cristo. And he dug himself out of a dungeon using nothing but a rusty pocket knife. And he was digging through solid rock. It took him thirty-seven years. He dug a hole so deep that when he came out, he found himself in China!"

I gave my side a confused scratch. "But Jim doesn't know anybody in China."

"That doesn't matter," Tom argued. "Looky, Huck, we'll need a rope ladder too."

"Why do we need a ladder if we're digging a tunnel?"

"Because that's the proper way to do things, Huck. Tomorrow you borrow one of Aunt Sally's sheets off the clothesline. We'll cut it up and make a ladder from it. Then we'll bake it inside of a pie that we'll have sent to Jim. I'm sure one of the slaves is taking him meals several times a day."

"Then what does Jim do with the ladder?"

"Nothing. He just hides it in his bed to be left behind. It'll be a clue that throws everyone off our trail."

That didn't make sense to me, but I trusted Tom knew what he was doing. So the next day I yanked one of Aunt Sally's sheets off the clothesline with my mouth. I also borrowed one of Uncle Silas's shirts because Tom said Jim could use it to write a letter on. Tom stole a spoon and some candles from the kitchen because he thought we could make a pen and some ink out of them. Don't ask me how.

That night, Tom and I slid down the lightning rod and slipped inside the storage shack. We worked for hours, digging at the dirt floor with a pair of rusty pocket knives. Those knives were worthless and we didn't get very far. Finally Tom said he reckoned it would be all right if I did my digging the way I knew best. So I set my front paws in motion, fast and furious.

In less than an hour, I had dug a tunnel into Jim's hut. Tom and I crawled through on our bellies. We came out, right underneath Jim's bed.

As I shook the dirt off my fur, I saw Jim sitting on the bed, watching us with amazement. By the light of a single candle, I noticed that one of Jim's legs was chained to one of the bed's legs. I jumped up on that bed and shook Jim's hand.

"I'm mighty glad to see you, Huck," Jim said. "I'm glad to see you too, Master Tom. If you boys will just help me get this chain off the bed leg, then I can climb through that tunnel you made."

Tom sat beside Jim. "No, Jim, we can't do it that way. It wouldn't be mysterious enough. I've got a plan all worked out. It might take a few weeks to pull off though. Just be patient."

"It took the Count of Monte Cristo thirty-seven years to escape," I said, trying to be helpful. "But you'll be out of here sooner than that."

"I hope so," Jim said, looking worried.

"Looky, Jim," Tom said. "You'll be receiving a pie in the next few days. Inside that pie you'll find a rope ladder made from sheets. Just hide the ladder under your mattress. We'll also be sneaking a shirt into you somehow. That shirt is for you to write a letter on. All prisoners have to write woeful letters. Say, does Uncle Silas ever come in here?"

"He comes every day to pray with me," Jim said, growing puzzled. "But I don't know how to write, Master Tom."

Tom waved a hand. "Don't worry about it. Just keep a lookout for that shirt. And make sure you check Uncle Silas's pockets when he comes tomorrow. I'll be slipping a spoon into one of his pockets that you can carve into a pen. I'll also be slipping some candles into your cornbread. We can find a way to turn those candles into ink."

Jim said he would do his best, even though he was certain he wouldn't be able to learn to write in the next few days.

The following morning at breakfast, Aunt Sally looked at Uncle Silas and said, "I've searched high and low but I can't seem to find your striped shirt. Did you do something with it?"

Uncle Silas was just a nice farmer fellow, a little on the meek side. He glanced down at his shirt and said,

"If it's not the shirt I'm wearing, I don't know where it could be."

I lowered my muzzle to my plate.

"It was hanging on the clothesline yesterday," Aunt Sally scowled. "Maybe a calf got hold of it. But that's not all that's gone. I'm also missing a sheet, a spoon, and six candles."

I choked on my food, fearing Tom and I were close to being caught. Aunt Sally was mostly a sweet lady, but when her fuse was lit, she had a real hot temper. Right then, I wished I was somewhere far away, like maybe Jerusalem.

"The calf must have taken the sheet too," Tom piped up.

Suddenly Uncle Silas fished something out of his pocket. It was a spoon that Tom had slipped in there only minutes before. Uncle Silas just stared at the spoon with a foolish expression.

Aunt Sally's jaw dropped open. "So you took the spoon. Silas, are you also hiding those candles in your pockets?"

"I've no idea how this spoon got in my pocket," Uncle Silas insisted. "But I can assure you there aren't any candles in my pocket. We've got a lot of rats in the cellar. Maybe they got hold of the candles."

"I bet that's it," Tom jumped in.

"Yeah, I bet that's it too," I added.

"Everybody, clear out of this kitchen!" Aunt Sally yelled, her finger aimed at the door. "That means you too, Tom and Sid. I need some peace and quiet because I feel like I'm losing my mind!"

None of us had to be told twice to scram. Tom decided to forget about making Jim write some woeful letters since we no longer had the spoon we needed for a pen. But we spent the entire day making the pie that would conceal the ladder.

First we tore the borrowed sheet into strips and fashioned a kind of ladder out of it. Then we went out to the woods and built a campfire. We stuffed the ladder and some flour and a few other things into an old tin pan. Then, with smoke floating all over, we baked that pie to a crisp. I've never met a piece of food I didn't like, but I didn't have much interest in that ladder pie.

That night, Tom and I crawled into Jim's hut.

"I got the pie this evening," Jim told us. "I took out the ladder and hid it under the mattress, just like you said."

Tom glanced around the dark room. "This dungeon looks too nice, though. Jim, do you have any rats in here?"

"No, sir," Jim said.

"All right, we'll get you some rats."

"But I don't want no—"

"Don't argue," Tom said, holding up a hand. "The escape won't be proper unless the dungeon is crawling with rats. It won't be so bad. You can train the rats and teach them tricks and maybe play music for them. Lots of prisoners have done that."

Jim just shook his head. "I tell you, I don't ever want to be a prisoner again. It's too much trouble."

I gave Jim a comforting pat with my paw. Even though we were causing Jim a lot of woe, I trusted that Tom knew the best way to plan the escape. I've never seen a boy with such a mind. Why, if I had Tom Sawyer's mind, I wouldn't trade it for anything, not even the chance to be a circus clown.

The next day, Tom and I trapped a whole mess of rats in the cellar. We put them in a wire cage, which he hid under Aunt Sally's bed. But when one of the Phelps children opened the cage, those rats went scurrying all over the house. As soon as Aunt Sally saw one, she jumped on a chair and screamed so loud it made my ears twitch for an hour afterwards.

Tom and I managed to catch most of the rats, but not all of them. For the next few days, one of them was always running up a wall or jumping onto a dinner plate or doing something ratlike. Aunt Sally was always whirling around, looking this way and that, imagining that another rat had scampered into the room.

"We still need to take a bunch of rats to Jim's dungeon," Tom whispered to me one night.

"Looky," I told Tom, "those rats have caused a lot of disturbance around here. Maybe we could just skip taking the rats to Jim and pretend that we did it."

After some grumbling, Tom went along with my idea. To be honest, I didn't like the rats much myself. Every time I saw one of those little furry fellows, my tail went quivering.

So . . . after three weeks of mighty hard work, everything was ready. But then Tom decided he wanted to throw in one last "finishing touch." Tom spent a long time writing a letter, which he slid under the door of the Phelps house. The letter read:

I wish to warn you that a gang of desperate pirates will be coming tonight at the stroke of twelve. They're coming to set free that runaway slave you've got locked up in the hut. I was one of the gang myself but I quit when I got religion. Now I wish to do the right thing and give you warning.

Unknown Friend

With a satisfied smile, Tom said this letter would make the escape even more exciting. I gave my side a nervous scratch, wondering if things might be getting a bit *too* exciting!

Meanwhile, back in Oakdale, I'm about to sacrifice my dignity . . . for a good cause, of course.

Chapter Twelve

Wishbone. *My name is Wishbone. Not Ralph. And not Popeye,* the terrier thought, staring down at the sailor suit. The white cap fell over one eye. *Proof that hats do not belong on dogs.*

Queenie stared at Wishbone, her pink tongue panting. She seemed to be having a good giggle at Wishbone's expense.

"Queenie, I'm warning you," Wishbone said in a low voice. "This is no time to start with me."

David bit his lower lip, looking uncertain. "The sailor outfit isn't bad. But Ralph could try another outfit before I make a final decision."

No! Not another outfit, David. Or Norton. Or whatever your name is, Wishbone insisted.

"We really have to go," Mr. Peabody said. "Just decide."

David held up the zebra-striped coat with the velvet collar. "Is this for male or female dogs?"

"Male—" Mr. Peabody answered.

"Female—" his wife said at the same time. Obviously they were in a hurry now.

"It's European," Wishbone said with a sigh. "Now get me out of this ship-ahoy gear and—"

Hearing the familiar sound of spinning wheels, Wishbone turned around. Joe and Sam were approaching on their bicycles.

Ah ha! Wishbone thought. *Lucky that Joe and Sam are close. Let's see . . . it's three kids and one dog against two grownups and one dog. But I count double, so—*

Joe and Sam pulled up beside the impromptu fashion show.

"Wishbone," Joe said, "we've been searching all over for you." He looked at David, then at the Peabodys. "Why is Wishbone wearing that—"

"Sorry, but this isn't Wishbone," David interrupted. "This is *my* dog, Ralph."

"What?" Sam stared at David. "What's going on, Da—"

"Norton," David said quickly. "You two are always forgetting my name. It's Norton. And this is my dog, Ralph. You know, the dog that people are always getting confused with Wishbone?"

"Listen to the cues," Wishone said, looking up at Joe and Sam, who still looked confused.

Sam spoke first. "What are you doing here . . . Norton?"

"Yes!" Wishbone said.

"I'm shopping. Sort of," David explained. "These people sell canine clothing."

"We've already met," Joe said, nodding at the Peabodys.

"I'm going to buy an outfit for Ralph," David told his friends. "But you know who would really flip for this stuff?"

"Who?" Joe asked.

"Mr. Krulla," David said, speaking the name very clearly. "He's always buying fancy things for his three cocker spaniels. Why don't you see if you can bring him over here?"

Ah, brilliant move, David, Wishbone thought. *Mr. Krulla is really Officer Krulla of the Oakdale Police Department.*

"You're right." Sam nodded thoughtfully. "Mr. Krulla will probably rush right over here. Come on, Joe, let's go get him."

Mr. Peabody raised a hand. "Listen, kids, my wife and I need to be on our way. Why don't you give me Mr. Krulla's full name and I'll make sure he gets one of our catalogs."

"No, his office is just around the corner," Joe said, pushing off on his bicycle. "We'll be right back with him."

Before anyone could respond, Joe and Sam were speeding away on their bicycles.

"I think Joe and Sam got the hint," Wishbone told David.

Mr. Peabody was no longer smiling. "What are you doing, son?" he asked David.

"I'm just trying to help you sell more clothing," David said, trying to act innocent.

Mr. Peabody's eyes grew dark. "What are you *really* doing?"

"Jack, take it easy," Mrs. Peabody whispered anxiously. "He's just a boy."

Wishbone moved between David and the Peabodys. "Hey, don't even think about trying anything on my buddy."

"Let's get out of here," Mr. Peabody told his wife as he quickly closed up the suitcase.

Mr. Peabody went to the green car, and Mrs. Peabody went to the blue car, with Queenie following her. The Peabodys didn't say goodbye or even ask for the sailor suit back. They obviously wanted to clear out —fast.

Officer Krulla won't be here for a few minutes, Wishbone thought. *I've got to somehow stop the Peabodys from getting away. What can I . . .*

Queenie had turned back for a last look at Wishbone. Her beady eyes seemed to say, "If you think I look silly in this tutu, you ought to see yourself in that sailor suit."

That's it!

With a sharp bark, Wishbone bolted straight for Queenie. A look of terror flashed in the poodle's eyes. Then she flew across the grass like a pink comet streaking through outer space. Wishbone charged after her, trying to look as ferocious as he could in a shiny blue sailor suit.

As Wishbone ran, he heard the voices behind him.

"Queenie, come back!" Mrs. Peabody called.

"Jenny, let's go," Mr. Peabody ordered.

"I can't leave Queenie!"

"Forget the dog. We have to get out of here!"

"Ralph won't hurt her," David said. "He's just playing."

As Wishbone flew after Queenie, the sailor cap sailed off his head. Wishbone bent back his ears, enjoying the feel of the rushing wind. Nothing matched the excitement of a good chase, and a poodle in a tutu was a better target than a stick or a cat.

I just have to keep chasing Queenie until the cops show up, Wishbone thought as he pumped his legs. *That should be any minute now. Oh, my mind is almost as brilliant as my feet are fast!*

As Queenie circled the pond, a few ducks turned to watch. Soon Wishbone was rounding the pond in hot pursuit. Up ahead Queenie leaped over a fallen log with the grace of a ballerina.

Hey, that wasn't bad, Wishbone had to admit. *Maybe that tutu is good for something after all.*

Wishbone glanced over his shoulder and saw that Mrs. Peabody was chasing after him now.

"Ralph, leave my Queenie alone!" the woman screamed, frantically waving her arms. "Bad dog, Ralph! Very bad dog!"

Glancing the other way, Wishbone saw Mr. Peabody climb into the green car. He slammed the door and started the engine.

Oh no, Wishbone thought, dodging an oak tree. *He's taking the green car. That's the car with the stolen goods in the trunk!*

Then a beautiful sound reached Wishbone's ears —the wail of a police siren.

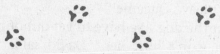

Hold on, before the cops come, we'd better check in on Huck and Tom and Jim. Come on!

Chapter Thirteen

The night of the big break-out arrived. Aunt Sally sent Tom and me to bed right after supper. She wouldn't tell us why. But we knew it was because she was worried about the desperate gang of pirates who were supposed to show up at midnight.

Around eleven o'clock, Tom and I slid down the lightning rod and sneaked to Jim's hut. We had borrowed some food for the escape, but Tom realized that we had forgotten the butter. Tom said that butter was real important and I should go back for it.

So I sneaked into the house's cellar and stuffed some chunks of butter in my straw hat. I heard a bunch of voices in the house. So I crept up the stairs and stole a peek inside the sitting room. About fifteen farmers were sitting around, each of them holding a gun. They looked fidgety and nervous, which made me realize they had come to fight off the gang of pirates. As they talked in low voices, I lifted my ears to hear the conversation. Something I heard made my fur bristle with fear.

I flew out of the house, dashed into the storage shack, crawled through the tunnel, and pulled myself up through the dirt floor of Jim's hut, which brought me under the bed. By now, Tom had gotten Jim dressed up in a lady's dress for disguise.

Panting hard, I said, "Tom, there's a whole mess of men waiting for the pirates. They've got guns. Real guns. And I heard them say that they're coming here. Right now. There's not a minute to lose!"

"Oh Lordy," Jim whispered.

"Ain't that bully!" Tom said, his eyes gleaming with excitement. "This is working out even better than I thought!"

Seconds later, we heard someone unlocking the hut's padlock. Tom, Jim, and I all dived underneath the bed. Just as a few of the men entered the hut, the three of us wriggled through the tunnel like a trio of snakes. We escaped into the shack before the men had realized what we had done.

"Is the slave in here?" I heard a man whisper.

"I can't tell," another whispered. "It's so awfully dark."

I peered outside, through a crack in the shack's wall. I saw the rest of the men spreading out across the plantation. When the men were far enough away, I signaled.

Tom, Jim, and I slipped through the door. Moving real quiet, we made our way to the fence. I grabbed the fence's cross-bar and climbed over. Jim came over next. Then Tom came over, but coming down he caught his pants on a big splinter. When Tom pulled his pants loose, the splinter gave a loud crack.

"Who's there?" a voice called through the darkness. "Answer or I'll shoot!"

We high-tailed it out of there as fast as our paws and feet would carry us. Suddenly—bang, bang, bang—bullets went whizzing over our heads.

"They're heading for the river!" a man shouted. "After em, boys!"

As Tom, Jim, and I ran, I could hear the boots of all the men tramping after us. My heart was beating so hard, I could almost hear that too. I had chased a few cats in my time and, gosh almighty, I began to understand how those cats felt.

I doubted the three of us would be able to outrun any bullets, so I steered us into a clump of bushes. It was a good idea, because soon the men went by without catching sight of us. Then we turned things around. We *followed* the men toward the river, moving fast but quiet.

In no time, I found the spot where I had hidden the raft. Tom, Jim, and I guided the raft into the middle of the water, Jim at the tiller, Tom and I using the poles. Keeping my ears high, I heard the men's boots and voices fading into the distance.

All three of us began grinning ear to ear. We had pulled off the escape!

"Huck and Master Tom," Jim said, waving his hands happily in the air, "I don't rightly know why your plan had to be so complicated. But I'm glad it worked!"

"What's the matter?" I asked Tom, who was examining his leg.

"I got shot by one of those bullets," Tom said, looking very pleased about it.

Jim and I rushed over and saw blood seeping through Tom's pants. Using my teeth, I tore a strip off a spare shirt, and Jim wrapped the strip around Tom's leg.

"It's nothing," Tom said, his face tight with pain. "Come on, man the raft. It's time we set sail for the seven seas!"

Jim shook his head slowly. "I'm not going anywhere until we get a doctor for Master Tom."

"If we fetch a doctor," I said, "it might ruin the escape. They might catch you again, Jim."

"I don't care," Jim said, placing a hand on Tom's shoulder. "If I have to wait forty years, I'm not leaving until we get a doctor for this wounded boy."

It was about the noblest thing I had ever seen. Jim was willing to give up his freedom just to help Tom Sawyer.

"Let me go for the doc," I told Jim. "When you hear the doc coming, you hide in the wigwam. Maybe he won't notice you."

"No doctor!" Tom protested. "We've got to escape! We've got to sail . . . sail the seven seas . . . and then we'll . . . "

Tom seemed to be getting dizzy and feverish. I untied the canoe from the raft, took the paddle, and rowed straight for the shore.

After asking around, I found the house of the local doctor. I explained to him that I had gone out fishing on the raft with my brother, but then my brother had a bad dream and accidentally shot himself in the

122

leg. The doctor said he'd go visit the boy, but that the canoe wasn't big enough for me, him, and his bag of supplies. So I told the doctor where the raft was located, and he climbed into the canoe by himself.

Weary from all the adventure, I curled up for a short nap on the ground. When I wakened, the morning sun was already warming my fur. I scratched at the doctor's door, but his wife told me that her husband hadn't gotten back yet. Fearing that Tom might be sick as a dog, I decided to swim out for the raft.

But soon as I stepped out of the doctor's yard, I ran into a pair of shoes that smelled awfully familiar. I looked up to see Uncle Silas staring down at me.

"Where have you been?" Uncle Silas said with a frown. "Your Aunt Sally has been worried sick about you and Sid."

"Uh . . . where have I been?" I scratched my side to stall for time. "Let's see . . . Sid and I went searching for the runaway slave. Finally we got so tired we went to sleep and we woke up just an hour ago. And Sid . . . well, Sid just went over to the post office to see if he could hear some news about the slave."

Uncle Silas made me follow him to the post office. Not surprisingly, Sid wasn't there.

So Uncle Silas took me home. Aunt Sally was so glad to see me, she wouldn't stop hugging and kissing me all over. But by the time night fell, there was still no sign of Tom or Jim or the doctor. I tossed and turned and scratched my fur all night long with worry.

Lo and behold, the next morning, Tom Sawyer came home in a blaze of glory. He was lying on a mattress that was being carried by the doctor and a group of men. Tom looked like a conquering hero at the head of a parade. Jim was there too, but I was sorry to see that his hands were chained behind his back.

"Oh, Sid is alive!" Aunt Sally cried with joy. "Thank God!"

"Looks like they've caught the slave too," Uncle Silas said, scratching his head.

Tom was taken to an upstairs bedroom, and Aunt Sally buzzed about like a bee, making sure Tom was comfortable. Tom was still feverish, though. His face looked red as a tomato and he kept babbling on about how he needed to sail the seven seas.

Meanwhile, the men took Jim back to the hut. This time they chained him up real good and they posted guards at the door. Some of the men thought that Jim ought to be hung for escaping. But some of the others argued against it, saying that it wasn't right to kill another person's property.

"Don't be overrough on him," the doctor advised. "When I found the wounded boy on the raft, I discovered I couldn't cut the bullet out without some help. And the boy was so sick, I couldn't leave him to go fetch anyone. I said to myself, 'I've got to have *help* somehow.' That very minute, the slave came crawling out of this wigwam and he said he'll help me fix the boy. And he did help me, quite a bit."

The doc explained that Tom had been so ill he couldn't be moved for a whole day. Then, that very morning, a group of men rowed by in a boat. The doc signaled them over and the men realized that Jim was the runaway slave. So they put Tom on a mattress, and they put Jim in chains, and they all came parading over to the Phelps plantation.

The next morning, I slipped into Tom's sickroom, but he was sleeping peacefully. Soon Aunt Sally and Uncle Silas entered the room. We were all glad because Tom's face didn't look so feverish anymore.

By and by, Tom opened his eyes and said, "Hello. Why, I'm at home. How did that happen? Where's Jim?"

I placed my front paws on the bed. "Everything is all right, Sid."

"Did you tell them about it?" Tom asked me.

"About what?" Aunt Sally asked.

I nudged Tom's hand. I was trying to signal him to keep mum about what we had done. But before I could stop him, Tom spilled the whole story about he and I had broken Jim out of the hut. He told how we had stolen the sheet, shirt, spoon, and candles and made the pie and dug the tunnel and all the rest. Tom told the story so fast and proud it seemed his tongue was spitting fire.

Uncle Silas scratched his head in confusion.

"Sid, you're too sick for me to punish you," Aunt Sally said, trying to control her temper. "And right now I'm just happy you're getting better. But I don't want either you or Tom meddling with that slave anymore."

"I thought you said everything was all right," Tom said, glancing over at me. "Didn't Jim get away?"

I shrugged.

"No, he didn't get away," Aunt Sally told Tom. "He's back in the hut, all locked up."

Tom shot bolt upright in bed. "They don't have any right to hold him prisoner! Turn him loose right now! He's not a slave anymore! He's as free as any creature that walks this earth!"

Aunt Sally looked at Uncle Silas. "I fear he's still out of his head with sickness."

"No, I'm not out of my head!" Tom protested. "Listen to me! Jim used to belong to Miss Watson. That's a lady in St. Petersburg that Hu . . . Tom and I both know. But Miss Watson died two months ago. And she was so ashamed that she was planning to sell Jim that she declared in her will that Jim should be set free. Jim is rightfully a free man!"

My ears shot up.

"Hold on a second," I told Tom. "If Jim was already free, why didn't you just say so? That means there was no need for him to have been a prisoner in the first place. You could have saved poor Jim, not to mention everyone else, a bunch of trouble!"

"I didn't say anything," Tom replied, "because I didn't want to miss all the grand adventures we had!

Why, if we had gotten away safe in the raft, I was planning for us to ride all the way down to New Orleans. Then I'd tell Jim he was free and we'd all ride back up the river in style on a steamboat. When we landed, there would be a brass band playing for us and we'd all be heroes! That was my pl—Aunt Polly!"

I whipped my muzzle around to see what Tom was suddenly staring at. Aunt Polly was standing in the doorway. She was Tom's aunt, the lady he lived with in St. Petersburg. All of us were so amazed to see her, you could have knocked us over with a feather.

Myself, I smelled trouble coming. Aunt Polly would soon find out that Tom and I weren't going by our real names. I found a nice spot for myself under Tom's bed.

"Tom," Aunt Polly said, adjusting her spectacles, "what in the world have you been up to?"

"Oh dear," Aunt Sally said with a worried look. "Has the fever changed him so much? That isn't Tom in the bed. It's Sid. Tom is . . . where is he? He was here just a minute ago."

"No, that's Tom in that bed," Aunt Polly stated. "I've been raising him enough years to know Tom Sawyer when I see him. And that's Huck Finn that slipped *under* the bed. Come on out, Huck."

I crept out, tucking my tail between my legs.

Aunt Sally looked pretty mixed up. Uncle Silas seemed dumbstruck.

Then Aunt Polly explained why she had shown up. "I was most confused when I got Sally's letters saying that both Tom and Sid had arrived safely. I knew that Tom had come alone, without Sid. I wrote you twice, Sally, asking what you meant by Sid being here. When I didn't get a reply I decided to come here myself. I wrote another letter saying I was on my way."

"Well, Polly, I never got any of those letters," Aunt Sally said, shaking her head.

Everyone turned to look at Tom.

"Tom," Aunt Polly said with a stern expression. "Where are those letters?"

"What letters?" Tom asked innocently.

Aunt Polly's face began to turn red.

"They're in the trunk," Tom confessed. "I didn't read them, but I guessed they might make some trouble for Huck and me. So I . . . just hid them away. They're good as new, though."

It looked like steam was about to blow out Aunt Polly's ears.

So Tom set about explaining everything. This time he backed up to the start, from the moment when I told Aunt Sally I was Tom instead of Huck. Finally, all the knots were untangled.

We had Jim out of his chains in no time. First thing Jim did was pay a visit to Tom in his sickroom. I was there too.

Tom gave Jim forty dollars for being such a good prisoner. Then Tom suggested that three of us slip out one night and go on some more grand adventures together.

"That suits me," I said with a wag of my tail. "Just so long as I don't have to meet up with my pap again."

Jim crouched down to me, real solemn. "Don't worry, Huck, you won't be seeing him no more."

"Why not?" I asked.

"Remember back on Jackson's Island when we saw that houseboat floating by?" Jim said quietly. "Remember how there was a dead man on board but I wouldn't let you look at him? That dead man was your pap, Huck. He's gone now, for good."

I lay down and rested my muzzle on my paws. All kinds of memories went floating through my head, like the currents of the river. Mostly I thought about all the different people and strange situations I'd come across lately. And it seemed all those things had made me into a slightly different person somehow. Or perhaps all those things just helped me understand the person I naturally was.

Jim looked at me, a real kind expression in his eyes. It seemed like he almost knew what I was thinking. He rubbed my head, but I'm not sure if he was doing it for good luck or to give me comfort.

So that's how things turned out. Pap, he was dead and wouldn't be bothering me no more. The Widow Douglas, the duke and king, Mary Jane —I never saw none of them again. Tom Sawyer, he soon got better and he wore the bullet that wounded him on a chain around his neck. By jings, Tom was awfully proud of that bullet.

As for Jim, he set off on his own, a free man finally. I had no doubt that he would find a way to buy the freedom of his wife and children. With all my heart, I hoped that Jim would find a heap of good luck in his life. He was the best friend I ever had.

Well . . . there ain't nothing more to write about, and I'm glad. If I had known how much trouble it was to make a book, I wouldn't have tackled it. My brain is sore from thinking and my poor paws are sore from writing.

I better get going now. I'm planning to head out by myself for the territory way off in the west. That's because Aunt Sally has a mind to adopt me and see that I get civilized. I couldn't stand that. I been there before.

Yours truly, Huck Finn

So Huck heads out west, and we all wish him great luck on his adventures. But let's not forget, we've got a pretty big adventure happening in Oakdale.

Chapter Fourteen

With a blaring siren and swirling red light, a police car pulled to a stop right behind Mr. Peabody's green car. Officer Krulla and his partner, Officer Edwards, sprang from their vehicle.

Making a wide U-turn, Wishbone left off chasing Queenie and ran for the police car. Just as Wishbone reached the parked cars, Joe and Sam rolled up on their bicycles.

Mr. Peabody now stood by the car, looking unhappy. At David's suggestion, the policemen made Mr. Peabody open the car's trunk. As the policemen quickly looked through the purse, Mrs. Peabody and Queenie joined the group. David identified Gilbert's Zip-T. Joe pointed out his mother's CD player.

Officer Krulla told them they were under arrest and read them their rights. Mr. and Mrs. Peabody nodded, looking as if they had been through this kind of thing before. Then, Officer Edwards handcuffed them.

"This wouldn't be happening if it wasn't for that

dumb dog of yours," Mr. Peabody grumbled to his wife.

"Don't you call Queenie a dumb dog," Mrs. Peabody shot back.

Officer Edwards helped the Peabodys and Queenie into the back seat of the car. Meanwhile, Officer Krulla spent some time talking on the car radio. Wishbone and the kids watched in stunned silence.

Soon Officer Krulla walked over to them. "David, thanks to you and your friends, we've caught two wanted criminals. Sergeant Ryan at the station just finished running a national check on them. Their real names are Jack and Jenny Thornhill. They're wanted in three states for their Canine Couture scam."

"Really?" David said with amazement.

"They go door to door with merchandise and get themselves invited inside," Officer Krulla explained. "At some point, when the residents are distracted, the lady wanders off and sneaks an item or two into her purse."

"That's exactly what they did at my house," David said.

Office Krulla nodded as he removed items from Mrs. Peabody's purse and set them on the trunk of the car. "They favor jewelry and electrical devices. Things that are small, valuable, and easy to sell. Like these items."

Joe pointed to a portable CD player. "My mom keeps that in her study."

"And this is Gilbert's Zip-T," David said, picking up the purple computer. "See? Here's Gilbert's name engraved on the back. Boy, am I glad to get my hands on this!"

"I bet you are," Wishbone commented.

"I have to take the stolen goods down to the station so we can make a complete report," Officer Krulla told the boys. "You can claim your items in about two hours. Is that all right?"

"Perfect," David said, giving a thumbs-up. "I'll have the computer back before Gilbert comes by to get it tonight."

The two police officers climbed into the cruiser, ignoring the couple arguing in the back seat. Queenie stared out the window at Wishbone. Her worried eyes seemed to say, "Do you know a good lawyer we can call?"

Oh, now I feel bad for Queenie, Wishbone thought as the police car drove away. *She's really not guilty of anything, except maybe a snobby personality. But that's pretty standard for a poodle.*

"Well," David told Sam and Joe, "I guess you guys got my hint about Officer Krulla."

A grin lit Joe's face. "When you told me Wishbone's name was really Ralph, I thought you'd lost it."

"But when you said *Mr.* Krulla might want some dog clothes," Sam added, "we began to get the picture."

"We called the police from the first pay phone we saw," Joe said, summing it up.

"They would have gotten away if it hadn't been for Wishbone," David said. "He distracted the Peabodys by chasing their poodle. You should have seen him go after her. It couldn't have been easy with this sailor suit on."

Oh yeah, Wishbone remembered. *I'm still wearing that embarrassing sailor suit. I just hope Joe and Ellen don't make me keep it.*

"Come on, boy," Joe said, kneeling down to the dog. "Let's take this outfit off, pronto."

"Oh, you're a fine one to talk," Wishbone told Joe. "You and Ellen were all set to buy me a full line of clothing from the Canine Couture collection. I heard it with my own ears. 'Oh, this jacket is so cool!'"

Joe helped Wishbone wriggle out of the sailor suit.

"Mom made me look at these dog clothes for about twenty minutes," Joe told his friends. "At first, I thought she was interested in buying something for Wishbone."

"She was!" Wishbone cried out.

"But she wasn't?" Sam asked.

"No, mom doesn't go for that stuff. After they were gone she explained that she was just being polite."

Wishbone tilted his head. "So you and Ellen weren't really going to deck me out in doll clothes?"

Joe crumpled the sailor outfit into a ball and sent it flying through the air as if it were a basketball. His aim was perfect: the outfit landed in a nearby garbage can.

"Nice shot," Sam said, patting Joe's arm.

"Yippee!" Wishbone yipped, running around in a joyous circle. "Free at last! Free at last!"

The dog dove to the ground and rolled around, enjoying the feel of the grass on his fur.

"Wishbone," David said, scratching the dog's back, "you deserve a big reward for everything you did today. I'm going to buy a box of dog treats to keep in my room. Every time you come by, you'll get one. Or two. Or maybe three."

"Terrific!" Wishbone bounced to his feet. "I like the liver-flavored kind. Well, I like the bacon-flavored, too. Maybe you should get both. In fact, let's hit the pet store right now!"

The three kids and Wishbone walked out of the park. The late afternoon sun angled through the trees, bathing Wishbone's fur with rays of warmth.

Doggie treats . . . warm sun . . . good friends. What's not to like? Wishbone thought, his tail whipping back and fourth. *David won't have to be grounded. And now and forever, I won't be wearing anything but a stunning white fur coat, decorated, of course, with well-selected spots of brown and black. Like Huck, I'm not up for being civilized. Not if it means wearing a pink tutu!*

By jings, this has been an exciting day. Let's see . . . I crossed paths with crooks and cops and a coffin, not to mention a runaway slave and a poodle in a pink tutu. And I think I even learned to spell "Mississippi." So next time you're feeling some need for some serious adventure, take a trip with my old friend, Huckleberry Finn!

About Mark Twain

Mark Twain led a life every bit as adventurous as that of Huckleberry Finn.

Born in 1835, Twain was actually named Samuel Langhorne Clemens. He grew up in Hannibal, Missouri, a port town located along the Mississippi River. In his late teens, he became a steamboat pilot, guiding steamboats up and down the river's winding path. Twain grew to know the Mississippi like an old friend and met all sorts of colorful "river characters." Later he would use the Mississippi as the setting for many of his stories.

As a young man, Twain fought briefly in the Civil War, then headed west to mine silver in Nevada. While out west he began writing humorous stories and newspaper articles, using the pen name of Mark Twain, a steamboat pilot's term for "safe water."

Eager to see the world, Twain traveled to Hawaii, Europe, and the Holy Land, then wrote a book about his travels called *Innocents Abroad*. Published in 1869, it brought the budding author instant fame and fortune. Twain married and moved to Hartford, Connecticut, where he had three daughters and produced a growing family of books.

In 1876, Twain published the very popular *Adventures of Tom Sawyer*. Immediately, he began working on a sequel but he took his time, letting it ripen into one of the freshest and most original books the world had yet seen. In 1885, he published this new book, his masterpiece—*Adventures of Huckleberry Finn*.

Later Twain lost most of his fortune when he invested in a newfangled type of printing press. To pay off his debts, Twain toured the globe, giving witty lectures and reading selections from his books. Famous for his white suit and mane of white hair, Twain became one of the most recognized personalities in the world.

About *Adventures of Huckleberry Finn*

A dventures of Huckleberry Finn is often called The Great American Novel. The honor is deserved.

Adventures of Huckleberry Finn is actually a sequel to Adventures of Tom Sawyer. It picks up where Tom Sawyer left off, and both books feature Tom and Huck. But the two novels are quite different in tone. Tom Sawyer is mostly a lighthearted piece of entertainment, while *Adventures of Huckleberry Finn* is something much deeper—a serious look at morality and character growth.

Few images in all literature match the power of Huck and Jim riding their raft down the Mississippi River. They are two outcasts from society, each searching for a place where he can be free to be himself. It's easy for the reader to imagine that he or she is also on that river, searching for his or her own personal freedom.

Perhaps the most striking feature of *Adventures of Huckleberry Finn* is the way it's told in Huck's own "voice"—as if Huck himself actually wrote the book. Since Huck is only a simple country boy, the writing has the natural feel of a real boy's speech, bad grammar and all. This book first introduced the idea that good literature didn't have to be written in a formal manner. Many books since have followed up on this idea. This is why the great author, Ernest Hemingway, claimed that, "All modern American literature comes from one book . . . *Huckleberry Finn.*"

However, not everyone appreciates *Adventures of Huckleberry Finn.* The book's naturalness has caused many critics and readers to label it "trashy." Furthermore, many people (perhaps mistakenly) feel that the book paints an unflattering portrait of African-Americans. For these reasons, it has been banned from many classrooms and libraries across the country. Even so, the novel has become one of the world's most beloved books, and it's been adapted numerous times into plays and films.

About Alexander Steele

Alexander Steele is a writer of books, plays, and screenplays for both juveniles and adults. He has written seventeen books for kids, covering everything from pirate treasure to snow leopards to radio astronomy.

Like many boys, Alexander felt an early kinship with Huck Finn. He first read *Adventures of Huckleberry Finn* in comic-book form, then soon moved on to the real book. What a surprise! The book was so funny and easy-going, it hardly seemed like a classic. And the book had special meaning for Alexander because he grew up in the South, at a time when blacks and whites were rather mistrustful of each other. Then and now, Alexander is still learning from Huck.

Alexander lives in New York City, which has several fashionable shops for doggie clothing.

WISHBONE Mysteries

Read all the books in the
WISHBONE™ Mysteries series!

❏ #1 *The Treasure of Skeleton Reef*
by Brad Strickland and Thomas E. Fuller

❏ #2 *The Haunted Clubhouse*
by Caroline Leavitt

❏ #3 *Riddle of the Wayward Books*
by Brad Strickland and Thomas E. Fuller

❏ #4 *Tale of the Missing Mascot*
by Alexander Steele

❏ #5 *The Stolen Trophy*
by Michael Jan Friedman

❏ #6 *The Maltese Dog*
by Anne Capeci

❏ #7 *Drive-In of Doom*
by Brad Strickland and Thomas E. Fuller

❏ #8 *The Key to the Golden Dog*
by Anne Capeci

❏ #9 *Case of the On-Line Alien*
by Alexander Steele

❏ #10 *The Disappearing Dinosaurs*
by Brad Strickland and Thomas E. Fuller

❏ #11 *Lights! Camera! Action Dog!*
by Nancy Butcher

❏ #12 *Forgotten Heroes*
by Michael Anthony Steele

❏ #13 *Case of the Unsolved Case*
by Alexander Steele

❏ #14 *Disoriented Express*
by Brad Strickland and Thomas E. Fuller

❏ #15 *Stage Invader*
by Vivian Sathre

❏ #16 *The Sirian Conspiracy*
by Michael Jan Friedman and Paul Kupperberg

❏ #17 *Case of the Impounded Hounds*
by Michael Anthony Steele

❏ #18 *Phantom of the Video Store*
by Leticia Gantt

❏ #19 *Case of the Cyber-Hacker*
by Anne Capeci

The Adventures of WISHBONE™

Read all the books in
The Adventures of Wishbone™ series!

- [ ] #1 *Be a Wolf!*
      by Brad Strickland
- [ ] #2 *Salty Dog*
      by Brad Strickland
- [ ] #3 *The Prince and the Pooch*
      by Caroline Leavitt
- [ ] #4 *Robinhound Crusoe*
      by Caroline Leavitt
- [ ] #5 *Hunchdog of Notre Dame*
      by Michael Jan Friedman
- [ ] #6 *Digging Up the Past*
      by Vivian Sathre
- [ ] #7 *The Mutt in the Iron Muzzle*
      by Michael Jan Friedman
- [ ] #8 *Muttketeer!*
      by Bill Crider
- [ ] #9 *A Tale of Two Sitters*
      by Joanne Barkan
- [ ] #10 *Moby Dog*
      by Alexander Steele
- [ ] #11 *The Pawloined Paper*
      by Olga Litowinsky
- [ ] #12 *Dog Overboard!*
      by Vivian Sathre
- [ ] #13 *Homer Sweet Homer*
      by Carla Jablonski
- [ ] #14 *Dr. Jekyll and Mr. Dog*
      by Nancy Butcher
- [ ] #15 *A Pup in King Arthur's Court*
      by Joanne Barkan
- [ ] #16 *The Last of the Breed*
      by Alexander Steele
- [ ] #17 *Digging to the Center of the Earth*
      by Michael Anthony Steele
- [ ] #18 *Gullifur's Travels*
      by Brad and Barbara Strickland
- [ ] #19 *Terrier of the Lost Mines*
      by Brad Strickland and Thomas E. Fuller
- [ ] #20 *Ivanhound*
      by Nancy Holder